Transformation

MARILYN KAYE

BANTAM BOOKS
NEW YORK • TORONTO • LONDON • SYDNEY • AUCKLAND

RL 5.5, 008–012
TRANSFORMATION
A Bantam Skylark Book / December 2000

ISBN 0-553-48716-7

Visit us on the Web! www.randomhouse.com/kids

Published simultaneously in the United States and Canada

Bantam Skylark is an imprint of Random House Children's Books, a division of Random House, Inc. SKYLARK BOOK and colophon and BANTAM BOOKS and colophon are registered trademarks of Random House, Inc. Bantam Books, 1540 Broadway, New York, New York 10036.

PRINTED IN THE UNITED STATES OF AMERICA

OPM   10   9   8   7   6   5   4   3   2   1

For Colette Moran

Transformation

one

On a bright, warm Sunday morning, the parking lot at Sunshine Square was getting crowded. Not with cars, though. Most of the mall's stores didn't open until later in the afternoon, so the shoppers hadn't arrived yet. The occupants of the parking lot were mostly seventh, eighth, and ninth graders from Parkside Middle School, and they didn't have cars. Their preferred modes of transportation were in-line skates and skateboards.

The only open stores were a bakery, a pharmacy, and a shop that rented out in-line skates along with helmets, kneepads, and other accessories. Amy Candler and Eric

Morgan were in that shop, picking up their rental skates for the morning.

The owner handed Amy a pair in her size, and she eyed them with dismay. "These brake pads look worn down," she complained. "I think they need to be changed."

The man pretended not to hear her. "You want kneepads?"

"Yeah," Eric said.

"Me too," Amy chimed in, although she doubted she would need them. It wasn't likely that she would fall, and even if she did scrape her knees, they would heal quickly. Which was precisely why she always wore kneepads. She didn't want anyone to see exactly how fast her cuts and bruises disappeared. It would be a clear indication that she was not your average twelve-year-old, seventh-grade, female human being.

She knew the man wouldn't even consider fixing the brake pads or exchanging her skates, so she accepted them as they were. Eric wasn't too thrilled with his pair either.

"These shoelaces are like threads," he grumbled as he sat on the store bench to put them on.

"I've got shoelaces in my backpack," Amy offered. She reached inside and took them out. The laces were hot pink, and Eric made a face.

"No thanks," he said. "I guess these will hold up for a couple of hours. Why are you carrying around pink shoelaces?"

"For trading, of course," Amy replied. "I've already got two pairs of pink ones, and I need light blue to go with my new T-shirt."

Eric had heard this kind of explanation before, but he still looked incredulous. "That is so lame, Amy. Why don't you just go out and *buy* a pair of blue shoelaces? They can't be all that expensive."

"Blue shoelaces are not easy to find," Amy told him. "Besides, buying them wouldn't be any fun."

Finding, collecting, and wearing shoelaces to match your clothes was one of the latest trends at Parkside. At that moment, light blue was among the most wanted colors, with kelly green a close second.

Eric wasn't into the shoelace fad. "It's so dumb," he asserted. "Shoelaces should be white, brown, or black."

"Says who?" Amy challenged. "And what's the difference between collecting shoelaces and collecting baseball caps? Remember *that*?"

Baseball caps had been huge back in the fall, and Eric had collected almost fifty. Now, months later, they were stuffed in a box in the back of a closet, since the cap fad was history. Amy figured that was the whole point of fads—they didn't last forever. There were clothing fads, like caps and shoelaces, and word fads, like when everyone said a good thing was "awesome." No one used that word anymore.

There were even food and drink fads. A few months ago, everyone had been chugging bottles of one particular iced tea flavor, orange-lime-kiwi. Now the traditional carbonated soft drinks were back in style. The latest edible fad was Cocodoodles, a chocolate ball coated with a lemon- or lime-flavored soft candy. You could suck on the sticky balls for ages till the candy part wore off, and then you chomped the chocolate. Your tongue would stay yellow or green for hours.

When she finished lacing her skates, Amy stood up and rolled out of the store onto the pavement. Eric was just behind her.

"These brake pads are definitely worn down," she declared. "I wish I had my own skates so I wouldn't have to rent any."

"Yeah, me too," Eric said. "I'm going to ask around, find out how much they cost." He took off, gliding across the parking lot toward a group of his ninth-grade basketball buddies. Amy skated around the rim of the lot and looked for some of her own seventh-grade friends.

She knew that her best friend, Tasha, Eric's sister, wouldn't be there. Tasha was never wild about sports fads. Amy herself loved the sensation you got from moving fast, and she hoped the in-line skating fad would go on for a long time. She liked it so much, she decided she just might go on skating after the fad had gone the way of baseball caps.

She had to swerve suddenly to avoid colliding with Alan Greenfield, a homeroom classmate who was fooling around on a skateboard, and she gave him a withering look. "Watch out, Alan," she yelled as she zoomed past him. Skateboards were so not cool anymore. Personally, she thought skateboarders should be banned from the lot so the inline skaters could rule.

But she couldn't complain about anything today. The sun was shining, and in just a few weeks school would let out for the summer. She didn't have any homework hanging over her head, she hadn't fought with her mother for at least a week, and she had a boyfriend to go skating with. Well, not exactly *with*—they would arrive and leave together, and that was about it. But that's the way boyfriends and girlfriends acted in middle school, and she wasn't about to try to change the rules. She popped a lemon Cocodoodle into her mouth and skated faster.

Actually, she wasn't that crazy about Cocodoodles. She thought they were too sweet, and they were so gummy they stuck to your teeth. But when it came to fads, she usually tried to go along with them. Not because she was a mindless follower—it was just that she didn't like to call attention to herself. She was already so different from everyone else, she didn't really need to isolate herself even more from her peers.

Like right that moment, when she was tempted to move *really* fast, to fly across the lot until she reached a vacant area and go into some rapid spins. That would feel great, so exhilarating, and everyone would be terribly impressed. But then they'd want to know how she could perform such extraordinary feats, and what was she going to tell them? The truth? That she was a genetically designed clone who had physical capabilities way beyond theirs?

"Amy!" a voice called out.

She identified the direction the voice was coming from and skidded to a stop in front of Simone Cusack and Linda Riviera. Both of them were in her math class at Parkside.

"Did you understand the homework assignment for tomorrow?" Simone asked in a plaintive voice.

Amy hedged. "I got *some* of it," she said. Just as she couldn't demonstrate her prodigious athletic skills, she tried not to show off how much more easily she could learn than most people.

Linda scrutinized her through tiny, hostile eyes. "I

don't suppose you'd consider sharing your answers with the rest of us."

Amy pretended Linda was joking. "Ha, ha, very funny. See ya."

She moved on, but she heard Simone moan, "I'll bet she aced it, she gets everything right in math."

And Linda responded with "I can't *stand* Amy Candler."

Linda spoke more loudly than Simone, and Amy was pretty sure she wanted Amy to overhear her. She could have saved herself the effort—Amy would have heard her even if she had whispered. That was part of Amy's genetic makeup too: She could see and hear better than regular people. Sometimes, like now, this ability wasn't a blessing.

It didn't ruin her good mood, though. There would always be nasty, snotty girls like Linda Riviera, and Amy didn't waste her time feeling bad because Linda didn't like her. On her next lap around the lot, she paused to talk to Layne Hunter and Carrie Nolan, two much nicer classmates. They were in the midst of an animated conversation and drew Amy right in.

"Amy, what's your opinion about Billy and Brianna?" Layne asked. "Do you think something's starting up between them? Carrie says yes, I say no."

"There's definitely something going on," Carrie

insisted. "Of course, what's really tragic is the fact that Jenny still thinks Billy's in love with *her*. Is she stupid, or what?"

"She just doesn't want to face the truth," Layne said sadly. "I feel sorry for Jenny. She's so sweet. But Billy is never going to think of her as anything more than a friend."

Amy was trying to recall classmates with those names, but no one came to mind. "Who are you talking about?"

The girls looked at her in surprise. "Jenny and Billy," Carrie said.

"And Brianna," Layne chimed in. "On *Cherry Lane*."

Now Amy got it, sort of. At least, she understood where the names had come from.

Layne and Carrie were talking about a TV show, a teen soap opera that everyone at Parkside was watching. At least, almost everyone. Amy was too embarrassed to tell them that she had never seen it. It came on at four-thirty every day, the same time as *Sunset*, another soap. Amy had been watching *Sunset* for years. No one else watched *Sunset*, and even Amy admitted that it had become very boring, but it was a habit.

She really had to force herself to break that habit, or learn how to program the VCR. It seemed like nowadays everyone was talking about the exploits of Jenny and Billy, not to mention Brianna, Tucker, Mitchell, and Danielle. Even though she'd never seen the program, Amy knew all the names from hearing them discussed in the hallways at school. *Cherry Lane* was now even bigger than *Dawson's Creek*.

"Well, what do *you* think, Amy?" Carrie wanted to know. "Are Billy and Brianna going to be the next big thing?"

Amy tried to remember what she'd heard about the show. Tasha was hooked on it, and she talked about it all the time.

Tentatively Amy said, "I thought Brianna and Tucker were a couple."

Layne was aghast. "Amy, that's ancient history. Where have you been?"

Amy was relieved that Eric chose that moment to circle around them and distract the girls from probing Amy's lack of knowledge too deeply. Eric was looking pleased with himself.

"Guess what?" he asked the group in general.

"What?" they all chorused automatically.

Eric dangled a little plastic bag filled with purple balls in the air. "Grape Cocodoodles!"

Layne let out a squeal. "Ooh, that's new! Where did you get them?"

"At the pharmacy," Eric said.

Layne and Carrie took off. "Want one?" Eric asked Amy. Without waiting for an answer, he handed her a grape Cocodoodle and skated away. Amy was still sucking on her lemon Cocodoodle. She couldn't spit it out, but the new grape Cocodoodle was already making her hand feel sticky. Quickly she made her way to a trash can, where she tossed the lemon ball and popped the grape one into her mouth.

She really should check out *Cherry Lane,* she thought. And as she made the decision, she noticed that some kids in the parking lot were wearing T-shirts that referred to the show or its characters. And as she continued skating, she noticed something even more interesting. A couple of girls she recognized as cheerleaders were talking to a girl named Tiffany Hull from Amy's phys ed class. Tiffany was a brain who was president of the debate club, and she didn't wear a bra yet, which basically put her in the category of nerd, at least in a cheerleader's mind.

"Personally, I think Brianna and Tuck are going to get back together," Amy overheard Tiffany telling the cheerleaders.

"I guess that's a possibility," one of the cheerleaders admitted. "But Brianna could do so much better. That Tucker is such a phony."

"But he's very cute," Tiffany reminded her.

Both the cheerleaders nodded fervently.

Amy watched and listened in amazement. *That* was something different. Not the Brianna and Tucker business—the fact that cheerleaders and nerds could find something to talk about. It was nice, she thought. Now she was even more committed to giving *Cherry Lane* a try.

On the way home, she asked Eric about the show. "Do you ever watch *Cherry Lane*?"

"I've seen it a couple of times," he admitted. "When I don't have basketball practice."

"Do you like it?"

He shrugged. "It's okay. It kind of grows on you, and you get into it. Want a grape Cocodoodle?"

Her hand still bore purple streaks from the last one he'd given her, but she took it anyway. "I wonder when Dr. Noble is going to get around to banning these." Their principal had a low tolerance for fads, and in the past she'd banned bubble gum and T-shirts with slogans from *The Simpsons*.

Eric considered the possibility. "Kids would just spit them out when she was around and put them back in their mouths when she wasn't looking. Just like they did with bubble gum."

"But it wouldn't be that easy," Amy pointed out. "These Cocodoodles color your tongue. You'd be carrying around the evidence that you'd just been eating one."

"I guess you'd have to keep your mouth shut," Eric said.

"But what if Dr. Noble started giving pop tongue checks?" Amy wondered.

When they arrived at their condominium community, they were both still laughing at the image of Dr. Noble storming unexpectedly into a classroom and ordering all the students to stick out their tongues. Then Amy noticed that a taxi had pulled into the driveway next to her own.

While the driver took suitcases out of the trunk, a woman with masses of frizzy red hair and trailing a long multicolored scarf swept toward the town house door. "Look, Monica's back," Amy announced.

The woman spotted her and Eric and waved.

"Where's she been?" Eric asked.

"She went to school for a month, somewhere up north around Big Sur. She's training to be an alternative therapeutic healer."

"A *what*?" he asked, but she was already running toward her neighbor.

"Monica, hi! How was your school?"

The woman gazed at her through kohl-rimmed eyes

that sparkled. "It was . . . I can't describe it. No words can capture the experiences I've just had. It was mystical, it was spiritual, it was . . . it was—"

"Sounds great," Amy said hastily, knowing that Monica would go on and on if she had the chance. "I like your new look." The last time she'd seen Monica Jackson, her neighbor had been into a gothic look, with spiky black hair, black lipstick, and a tattoo of a skull and crossbones on her arm. A temporary tattoo, of course, since Monica changed her look almost as often as most people changed their underwear.

"I think it suits my new profession," Monica told Amy solemnly. "It's less threatening, more open and nonconfrontational. Don't you think so?"

Basically, in the gauze dress and beads, Monica looked like a cross between a hippie from the 1960s and a New Age astrologer, so Amy had to agree it was a friendlier look than the last one, which had been almost scary.

Amy's mother must have witnessed Monica's arrival from a window. She came out onto the front steps and waved.

"Welcome home," Nancy Candler called out. "How was the school? Are you an official alternative therapeutic healer now?

"Yes, I am!" Monica said happily. "Oh, Nancy, it was . . . it was . . . indescribable, like something out of this world, like an experience in a dream, like—"

Nancy was also familiar with Monica's tendency to talk incessantly. "You can tell us all about it later," she said hastily. "We're having a picnic this afternoon, around three, and I've got to make potato salad. See you there!"

"You're coming to the picnic, aren't you?" Amy asked Eric.

"Sure," he said. "Hey, Amy—"

"Hmm?"

"What's an alternative therapeutic therapist?"

Amy looked at him reprovingly. "Oh, Eric, come on. Are you serious? Where have you been?"

"C'mon, help me out," Eric said urgently. "I don't want to look stupid at the picnic when everyone's talking about it. *Tell* me, what's an alternative therapeutic healer?"

Amy grinned. "Eric, I don't have the slightest idea."

two 2

Enticing smells wafted from the Candlers' terrace grill, and the picnic table displayed bowls of potato salad, cole slaw, chips, and macaroni salad. Dr. Dave Hopkins arrived with his specialty, double-chocolate brownies spiked with chocolate chips and covered with white chocolate icing. Tasha and Eric's mother produced a strawberry cheesecake.

Tasha arrived with a box, but the contents weren't edible. "I found some shoelaces at a flea market this morning," she told Amy excitedly. "Plaid! And I made some trades yesterday. Wanna look?"

"Yeah, I'll go get mine," Amy said, but she had something to do first. Eric had just given her a signal. It was time to hit up the parents for skates.

They had debated over when to approach their parents. Amy had suggested waiting until the last minutes of the cookout, when her mother would be more relaxed because the event had been a success. Eric vetoed that idea because he said his parents were never in very good moods after a great meal. They moaned and groaned about how they'd eaten too much and would have to go on a diet immediately.

So Amy and Eric had settled on the moment when people began to eat. Eric was heading toward his father, and Amy went to her mother.

She began with a compliment. "Everything looks great, Mom. And I just tasted your potato salad. It's the best ever!"

"Thanks, sweetie," her mother said happily. She gazed around at the group, which included a couple of neighbors and a colleague from the university where she taught. People were mixing nicely as they dug into the feast, and Nancy looked pretty pleased with herself.

So Amy plunged in. "Mom, I need my own in-line skates. The ones I rent are really crummy. They don't fit right and the brake pads are always worn. I don't even think they're safe to wear. Can I get my own?"

"Of course you can," her mother said promptly.

Amy's heart leaped.

"If you use your own money," her mother added.

Amy's heart plummeted even faster than it had risen. "Mom, they cost at least a hundred dollars! I don't have that much saved up."

"Then you'll just have to save some more," her mother replied. "Hi, Monica, I'm glad you could come!" She moved away from her daughter to greet the guest, and Amy stomped off to tell Eric the bad news.

From the look on Eric's face, she immediately knew he hadn't received a positive response either. "My dad says I have to buy them myself."

"Same for me," Amy said. Was it possible that the parents had anticipated the request and decided to form a united front? It didn't matter. "How much money do you have?" she asked Eric.

"Sixty-four dollars," he said glumly.

"I've only got forty-eight."

"Maybe there are sales," Eric mused. "Or I can ask around and see if there are any good secondhand skates. You'd better let me have your money, because if I find any, I'll have to buy them right away."

Amy agreed. She went back into the house to get the money she had stashed in a dresser drawer, and she also picked up her shoebox full of laces. Back outside, she turned her wad of cash over to Eric, collected her food, and joined Tasha on a bench to go over their shoelaces.

"I've got an extra pair of hot pink," Amy offered.

"No thanks, I never wear pink. You got any blue laces?"

Amy searched through the box. "Here's some navy ones. I'm looking for light blue."

"I don't have any light blue," Tasha said. "But I'll trade you olive green for the navy."

"Deal," Amy said.

Trailing the scent of musk and a scarf with a heavy fringe, Monica floated over to them. "What are you two doing?"

"Trading shoelaces," Amy told her. "Isn't this a great color?" She dangled the pair of hot pink ones in the air. Would she ever be able to get rid of these?

Clearly, Monica was not a potential trader. "Pink . . . it's not a very inspiring color. You don't happen to have any orange shoelaces, do you?"

"No, no orange ones," Amy told her. She realized that Monica was dressed entirely in various shades of orange.

Tasha noticed too. "Is that your new favorite color, orange?"

Monica smiled. "It's my color for today. My stomach's been upset."

Amy and Tasha exchanged confused looks, making it clear that they didn't get the connection, and Monica went on to explain. "Orange is a very healing color. It will help to neutralize the acids in my stomach."

Amy was doubtful. "Really? How can it do that?"

"Our bodies are very responsive to colors," Monica told her. "There was a wonderful lecture about that at the Institute of Being Well. Did you know that color can be just as important in therapies as aromas are? For example, if you are feeling tired, yellow can make you more alert. Yellow is also an enlightening color. It can provide clarity and increase the level of understanding. Of course, if you want true perception and wisdom, you need to wear purple."

Tasha fingered the laces she'd just received from Amy. "What can navy blue do for you?"

"It promotes serenity," Monica informed her. "It's very good for insomnia. But a small item like shoelaces won't have much power. You need to drench yourself in a color before it can have any real impact on your health."

Monica had been speaking loudly, and by now others were listening, including Dr. Hopkins, whom Amy and her friends now called Dr. Dave. He looked troubled. "Good grief, Monica, you don't really believe that colors can cure illnesses, do you?" he said.

"I certainly do," Monica replied indignantly. "Maybe *all* health problems can't be resolved through the use of color, but colors have been proven to impact a person's mood, and it's been proved that a mood can influence an illness. And I'm not the only one who believes this! Many intelligent people acknowledge the medicinal powers of color, as well as aroma, and music, and art. You medical doctors think the world of health is limited to surgery and prescription drugs. I plan to use alternative therapies, like meditation and hypnosis, in my practice."

Dr. Dave looked like he could use some therapy right that minute. He was clearly horrified. "Your *practice*? You're going to treat real live *patients*?"

"I certainly am," Monica said. "I've already had cards printed up." She produced a bunch of them and started handing them around.

" 'Monica Jackson, Healer,' " Dr. Dave read aloud. He groaned.

Monica ignored him. "Amy, the next time you have a tummyache, or a headache, you come see me before you take any pills."

"Okay," Amy said, though she never got headaches or stomachaches.

"You too, Tasha," Monica said. "And I want you guys to tell your friends about my practice. According to my teachers at the institute, word of mouth is the best way to get a practice like this going."

"Why don't you make some signs?" Amy suggested. "We could help you put them up."

"Good idea," Monica said. "I'll do that today."

Now Dr. Dave was looking seriously concerned. "Hang on there. Monica, what you're doing could be dangerous!"

"You're being too dramatic, Dave," Nancy scolded him. "What Monica wants to do won't hurt anyone."

"That's right," Mr. Morgan piped up. "I've heard of these New Age healers. Monica's just going to wave her hands around and chant incantations. That won't make people any sicker than they already are."

Monica wasn't pleased with his defense. "I do *not* plan to cast spells on people!" she declared hotly. "I am not a witch! I can help people."

Dr. Dave wasn't convinced. "But if people truly believe you can help them, they might not go to see a *real* doctor."

Monica was getting red, which was a dangerous sign.

"Oh, excuse me, I forgot that a *real* doctor is so wonderful," she said sarcastically. "He sticks needles in his patients and cuts them open and fills their bodies with toxic chemicals, and—"

Nancy jumped in to break the rising tension. "Okay, okay, no more arguments at my cookout, okay? Has everyone tried Dave's brownies? I think they can cure anything that ails you."

The lure of the brownies broke up the discussion. Eric made a hasty trip to the table to collect a plateful and brought them back to the bench where Amy and Tasha were still going through the shoelaces.

"You know," Tasha said, "when Brianna had that rash on her face, she thought Danielle had cast a spell on her."

"Danielle's a witch?" Eric asked with interest.

"Oh no, nothing like that. Brianna was just imagining things." Tasha grinned. "But I'll bet Jenny would call Danielle a word that *rhymes* with *witch*. Didn't you see how Danielle was flirting with Billy all last week?"

"I don't think that means anything," Eric declared. "Danielle talks like that to all the guys."

At least Amy figured out what they were talking about. "Eric, I thought you said you've only seen *Cherry Lane* a couple of times."

Eric gave her an abashed grin. "Well, I guess maybe I've seen more than two episodes. Tasha's been taping them for me when I have basketball practice. Like I said, it grows on you."

"You *have* to start watching it, Amy," Tasha insisted.

"Yeah, okay, I will," Amy said. "Who wants some cheesecake?"

But Tasha couldn't be distracted with cheesecake. "I'm *serious*, Amy," she said urgently. "I can't bear the thought that you don't know what's going on. This show is so unbelievably fabulous. You're my best friend, and I want to be able to talk with you about *Cherry Lane*."

"Okay, I'll watch it, I promise," Amy said.

"Today," Tasha ordered.

"This is Sunday," Amy pointed out. "The program isn't on today, is it?"

"I've got tons of tapes," Tasha assured her. "And I don't mind watching them again." She giggled. "I've probably already seen every episode three times already. One more time won't kill me."

So when the cookout was over and guests were beginning to leave, Amy went with Tasha and Eric to their house next door. Tasha pored over her tapes and selected one. "All the episodes from last week are on this tape," she told Amy.

Amy looked at her in alarm. "Tasha, I don't want to sit through five hours of *Cherry Lane!*"

"We'll just watch Friday's episode," Tasha said. She put the tape into the VCR, turned on the television, and pressed Play on the remote. Then she sat down on the sofa with a look of blissful anticipation on her face.

Suddenly her expression changed dramatically. The screen began to flicker wildly until it was a kaleidoscope of random colors. The picture was too wavy and distorted to view. The sound was strange too, slow and groaning like the way a cassette on a Walkman sounds when the battery is almost dead.

"Eric!" Tasha wailed. "Do something!"

For once, Eric actually obeyed his sister. He hurried to the TV set and began fiddling around with buttons and dials. Nothing changed on the screen. He punched a button that stopped the tape, and the regular TV program of the moment came on. "It's the VCR," he announced. "I think it's dead."

Tasha leaped up and hit the Eject button on the machine. The videocassette popped out. "I hope it didn't damage the tape," she said worriedly. "Come on, let's go over to Amy's and watch it."

At Amy's, Nancy Candler was still sitting out on the terrace with Dr. Dave, talking and having something to drink. Amy looked longingly at the big bowl of punch that was still on the table. It was such a pretty day, it was a shame to spend it indoors.

But Tasha was clearly determined that Amy was going to watch this show, so they all went inside. What surprised Amy was the fact that Eric was going along with all this. On such a sunny day, he was usually over at a basketball court. But he seemed willing, even eager, to see these episodes too.

Tasha gave Amy the tape, and Amy put it into the VCR. But it took her a while to figure out how to make the tape play. "It's a new universal remote control," she explained to the others. "It's really complicated." Finally she gave up and just hit the Play button on the VCR.

"Turn it up, turn it up," Tasha insisted as they heard the first strains of the opening music. Amy obliged and settled back on the sofa to see what all the fuss was about.

The scene opened with a close-up of a girl with skin so flawless it looked like porcelain. Her golden blond hair hung to her shoulders. The camera moved back, and Amy could see that the girl was walking down an empty hallway in what looked like a school. Every few seconds, she peeked through the window in a classroom door, then moved on.

"That's Brianna," Tasha announced. Amy could hear the excitement rising in her voice.

Brianna was now walking past a rest room. She paused and put her head against the door. Apparently she heard something going on inside, because she pushed the door open and went in.

"Jenny! I've been looking all over for you!"

Another porcelain girl, but this time with long brown hair, leaned against the wall, weeping hysterically. Brianna rushed to her side and embraced her. "What happened, Jenny?"

The brunette spoke through her sobs. "It's Billy. I asked him if he would take me to the prom. He said he already has a date!"

"Oh, Jenny," Brianna said sympathetically. She took some tissue and handed it to Jenny. "I'm so sorry. Who is he taking?"

Jenny wiped her eyes. "I don't know. Do you think he could have asked that new girl?"

"Danielle?" Brianna shook her head. "No, he doesn't like her; he told Tuck she's too pushy."

"You're so lucky to have a boyfriend like Tuck," Jenny said. "He's so nice, and he loves you so much. You know you'll have a date for the prom and for anything else that comes along."

"Yes," Brianna said. "Yes, Tuck is wonderful. I'm very lucky." The camera moved in for a close-up of her expression. Her eyes had a sad, faraway look, making it clear that she didn't really feel lucky at all. Then the picture faded and changed to a commercial.

"I'll see if I can fast-forward," Amy said, picking up the new universal remote. When Tasha didn't respond, Amy looked at her.

Tasha's eyes were glazed over. "Poor Jenny," she murmured. "Every time I see this scene, I want to cry."

"Really?" Amy looked at Eric. *He* didn't look like he was about to cry, thank goodness. But he was staring at the screen with a thoughtful expression that Amy had rarely seen on his face.

"She should tell Billy how she feels about him," he said.

Tasha disagreed. "That won't do any good. It'll just be embarrassing for both of them, and they won't even be good friends anymore."

"But at least she'll know where she stands," Eric pointed out.

"She doesn't want to know," Tasha said sadly. "She'd rather live with her fantasies."

"Well, that's stupid," Eric declared. "If she goes on believing that Billy is her one true love, she'll never be able to find a good relationship."

Amy couldn't believe what she was hearing. Her friends were talking about these characters as if they were real people in real life. And she didn't think she'd ever heard Eric use the word *relationship* before. "Uh, you guys want anything to drink?" she asked. "Or some cheesecake?"

"Shhh," Tasha hissed. "It's starting again."

Amy was about to point out that she could put the tape on Pause, but she didn't think that would do any good. Tasha was practically on the edge of her seat, almost as if she'd never seen the episode before. Amy didn't get it.

She continued not to get it as the show progressed. In the next scene, Brianna was walking in a park with a lanky, long-haired boy. They were holding hands.

"Do you know who Billy is taking to the prom?" she asked him.

"No."

"Oh, come on, Tuck. You're Billy's best friend, you have to know who he asked."

Tuck shrugged. "He might have asked Leslie Dial. I saw him talking to her after school yesterday."

"Leslie Dial! I didn't know Billy was interested in her. When did this happen?"

"Brianna, I don't *know*," Tuck replied irritably. "Why are you always asking me about Billy?"

"I'm asking for Jenny."

"She still thinks Billy is her one true love, doesn't she?" Tuck shook his head. "She's never going to be able to have a relationship with anyone else if she goes on like this."

"Well, you know how she feels about Billy," Brianna said.

Tuck stopped walking and took her shoulders, turning her to face him. "I know how Jenny feels about Billy. Everyone knows how Jenny feels about Billy. But now what I want to know is . . . how do *you* feel about Billy?"

"Oh, Tuck, don't be silly," Brianna said. "Come on, I'm thirsty. Let's get something to drink."

Amy stood up. "That sounds good to me. Who else wants something to drink?"

"Shhh—sit down!" Tasha shrieked. "Look!"

Amy looked. Brianna and Tuck had left the camera's range, and the focus was now on a huge tree. From behind the trunk, a petite girl with short red hair emerged. She was looking in the direction that Brianna and Tuck had gone in. And she was smiling in a way that wasn't very pleasant.

The picture faded and another commercial came on. "You see!" Tasha cried out triumphantly to her brother. "Danielle is definitely interested in Tuck."

"You can't be sure about that," Eric argued. "Maybe she was just interested in what they were saying about Billy."

"No way, Billy's not her type. What do you think, Amy?"

Amy was utterly bewildered. "I don't know. I haven't even seen this Billy yet."

"He'll be coming up in the next scene," Tasha assured her. "Don't worry, once you start watching *Cherry Lane* regularly, you'll catch on. And you'll get into it like everyone else."

Amy slumped back in her seat. "If you say so." She had her doubts. And she was remembering what Monica had said earlier about headaches. Amy didn't know what a headache felt like. But there was a funny little twinge just between her eyes, and she thought that might be what it was called. Because if there was anything that could give her a headache, it would most likely be *Cherry Lane*.

three 3

Amy wasn't alarmed when Tasha arrived alone the next morning for their regular walk to school. Eric was famous for oversleeping, especially on Monday mornings. His frequent tardiness accounted for his many periods in detention.

What did alarm Amy was the expression on her best friend's face. Tasha was obviously very upset about something. She was unusually pale, and her red eyes indicated that she had been crying. From the way her lower lip was trembling, Amy thought she looked like she was about to burst into tears again.

Amy was concerned. "What's the matter?"

Tasha's voice was shaky. "My mother . . . she made an appointment at the dentist for me. At four-thirty."

Now Amy understood Tasha's misery. Tasha had a notorious fear of dentists, and she went into a panic every time she had to see one. Even so, her reaction seemed a little extreme, way beyond her usual tense feelings about dentists. Was something else going on?

There was. "I'm going to miss *Cherry Lane*," Tasha continued in despair. "And I can't tape it because our VCR is broken! Amy, what am I going to do?"

Amy was taken aback by the outburst. Tasha was acting like she was on the verge of a nervous breakdown! Amy thought about the soap operas she herself had been semiaddicted to. "It's on every day, Tasha," she comforted her friend. "You know how these shows work—every problem gets dragged on forever. You won't miss much."

But this reassurance did nothing to ease Tasha's mind. "I don't care! I don't want to miss one word!"

"Calm down!" Amy ordered her. "Look, if it means that much to you, *I'll* tape it."

Tasha immediately brightened. "You will?"

"I'll set the VCR right now," Amy told her.

Tasha came inside to make sure Amy set the tape to record the right channel at the right time. Amy still didn't have total confidence in operating the new remote control, but she thought she'd gotten it right.

"C'mon, we have to hurry or we'll be late for school," she told Tasha. Actually, Amy didn't ever have to be late. With her superior physical constitution, she could speed up her walk or run and get there in plenty of time. But Tasha wouldn't be able to keep up with her—no regular human being would. Amy would have to walk at Tasha's pace and just hope they'd make it on time. Staying after school for detention was a pain.

They were in luck that morning, though. Just as they passed Monica's house, their neighbor was coming outside. "Hi, you guys want a ride to school?"

They piled into the car, and Monica handed them a sheet of paper from the stack she was carrying. "How does this look?"

Amy read aloud from the announcement. " 'Are you feeling tense, nervous, frightened? Do you have health problems that cannot be healed by ordinary doctors? Do you have a condition that cannot be cured with ordinary medicine? Are you interested in alternatives? Many illnesses are caused by stress, and treating the stress may cure the illness. I can treat your troubles, your fears, your stress-related illness with color, aroma, music, art, meditation, and hypnosis. Free consultation, by appointment only. Monica Jackson, healer.' " This was followed by Monica's phone and fax numbers, as well as her street and e-mail addresses.

"Notice the color combination I used on the signs," Monica said. "Orange, for healing, of course. And turquoise. That's a color that encourages impulsive actions. Lots of shops use turquoise-colored signs, to get people to buy stuff they've never even thought about buying."

"That's kind of creepy," Amy commented. "I mean, it's sort of like mind control, isn't it?"

"In a way," Monica admitted. "But I don't think a little mind control is a terrible thing. Not if it makes people happier and healthier. Do you guys think you could put a sign up at your school for me? Teachers and students are under a lot of stress. They need my help."

Amy wasn't so sure about that, but she agreed to take a sign. Thanks to Monica, the girls arrived at school early.

"Am I supposed to get permission to put up a sign?" Amy wondered out loud. Tasha didn't reply.

"Tasha, do you know the rules for putting up signs?" Still no response. "Tasha!"

"What?"

"Where *are* you? I've been asking you a question."

"Oh, sorry. I was just thinking . . . I have this feeling Brianna and Tuck are going to break up today."

Amy sighed. How long would this manic enthusiasm go on? She had her own favorite shows, of course. Like *Buffy the Vampire Slayer* and *Real World* on MTV. Those were favorite shows of Tasha's, too, and they tried to watch them together every week. They even talked about what happened on the shows. But neither of them had ever been this crazy about a TV show before.

It turned out that Tasha had no idea whether Amy needed permission to put up Monica's sign. Since there was time to kill before homeroom, Amy decided to go to the principal's office and ask.

The secretary told her she'd have to ask Dr. Noble, but there were people in Dr. Noble's office, so Amy had to wait. She sat down on a bench, and with nothing else to do, she found herself listening to the conversation that was going on behind the closed door.

It wasn't very interesting. A teacher was complaining about student behavior. Amy imagined that was what teachers talked about most of the time.

"They're constantly sucking on those awful candies. Cocodoodles, they're called. It's becoming an addiction!"

Dr. Noble wasn't upset. "Good grief, we're not talking about drugs," she said. "It's just candy."

"But it can't be good for their teeth. Not to mention the fact that the kids are dropping them all over the place, and people step on them. I've got smashed Cocodoodles on the soles of all my shoes! Can't you please ban them?"

"I don't think so," Dr. Noble said.

"Why not?" the teacher asked. "You banned that nasty bubble gum, and we don't have that around anymore."

"The bubble gum was a serious nuisance," Dr. Noble said. "The loud smacking made too much noise, and students couldn't hear their teachers. But Cocodoodles— well, we can order the students to stop dropping them on the floor, but that's all I'm willing to do."

"But why?" the teacher persisted. "We've banned other kinds of food, and certain T-shirts, and baseball caps. Why won't you ban Cocodoodles?"

"Because Parkside is aligning itself with a new educational program," Dr. Noble explained. "All the middle schools in the state are getting involved. It's very exciting. I'll tell you more about it at the faculty meeting today."

The teacher wasn't satisfied, and she wasn't willing to wait until the faculty meeting to get an answer. "I don't understand. How can a new educational program involve candy?"

"It's called Positive Control," Dr. Noble explained. "PC for short. The premise is not to waste time and energy fussing about trends and fads that can't really hurt the students. Banning something only turns it into a forbidden pleasure. With teenagers, our chief concerns should involve keeping them away from drugs, alcohol, violence, and any sort of behavior that can put them in danger."

Amy could hear the rustling of papers, and then Dr. Noble spoke again. "Positive Control puts out a list of approved trends and fads that we shouldn't try to ban. Here, you can see that Cocodoodles is listed. There are also lists of recommended movies and TV shows, and the show all the kids seem to be watching now is listed."

"*Cherry Lane,*" the teacher said. "I've seen it. It's total drivel, absolutely worthless."

"But harmless," Dr. Noble said. "And according to Positive Control, we should reserve our prohibitions for activities and experiences that can actually hurt kids."

It sounded like a good philosophy, Amy thought. Then she noticed the clock on the wall and realized she had exactly one minute to get to her homeroom. She couldn't wait around any longer in the hope of getting permission from Dr. Noble to put up the sign.

As she hurried to her homeroom, she passed the bulletin board where announcements were posted. Hastily she tacked Monica's paper to the board. If Dr. Noble didn't want it to be there, she could always take it down. Then she raced down the hall to her homeroom.

The homeroom routine was always pretty much the same. Unless there was a substitute or a fire drill, there were never any surprises. As soon as the bell stopped ringing, Ms. Weller would begin taking roll. Usually while she was calling out their names some dawdlers raced in. They would beg not to be counted as tardy so they wouldn't have to stay after school for detention. Sometimes Ms. Weller agreed, sometimes she didn't— she based her decision on how frequently each particular student had been guilty of this crime in the past. However, if you tore into the room after she had finished the roll call, you were definitely marked for detention—and someone always was.

When roll call was finished, the intercom would come on and morning announcements would be made to the entire school, by the principal, the assistant principal, or the secretary. After the announcements, Ms. Weller would hand out forms or collect forms or whatever was necessary. Then, if there was any time left, and if Ms. Weller was in a good mood, she'd tell the students they could talk quietly. After thirty seconds she'd tell them they were talking too loudly and that they had to keep the conversation level down to a dull roar. Fifteen seconds later she'd warn them again. Finally she'd tell them to stop talking and read silently until the bell. For almost ten months in the seventh grade, the routine hadn't varied.

Today the routine began normally, with the roll call. It was unusual, though, that no one came running in as Ms. Weller called out the names, and it was even more unusual that everyone was present.

Three short bells indicated that the intercom was on, and the voice of the secretary could be heard. "Good morning, boys and girls. May I have your announcements for the morning attention?"

There wasn't anything bizarre about that statement. The secretary was famous for mixing up words that way. What was unusual was the fact that Alan Greenfield, class clown, didn't make a joke about it. Nobody even laughed.

Ms. Weller looked both surprised and pleased. "Very good, class. You're actually beginning to show some signs of maturity."

There was nothing interesting in the announcements, just the usual reminders about overdue library books and extracurricular activities. Ms. Weller handed out forms for students to fill out if they wanted to order a yearbook, and then she told them they could talk quietly.

That was when Amy noticed another little change from the routine. There was some talking, of course, and Cocodoodles changed hands, but it was actually quiet in the room. And the soft buzz of conversation didn't escalate. Not once did Ms. Weller have to yell at them to keep the noise down.

Amy wondered if the constant sucking and chewing on Cocodoodles kept everyone's mouths too occupied for them to say much. A wild thought occurred to her—maybe Cocodoodles were the result of an educational conspiracy to keep students quiet! That could be the real reason why they were on the Positive Control "approved" list!

She had to tell Tasha her notion. Tasha was always saying that Amy wasn't creative, and Amy was pleased with herself for coming up with this crazy idea. This was the kind of subject that would make a funny article for the school's paper, *The Parkside News*.

As the morning progressed, Amy began to wonder if her crazy theory was really so crazy after all. In halls and in classrooms, students were less rowdy than usual. Amy decided this had to be a Monday thing. Maybe everyone was tired from having stayed up late on the weekend. Funny how she'd never noticed this before.

Even so, she couldn't wait to tell Tasha her Cocodoodle Conspiracy idea. Tasha would compliment her on her creativity, and they'd have a good laugh.

But when Amy arrived at the cafeteria for lunch, she could see immediately that Tasha wasn't going to be receptive to jokes about Cocodoodles or anything else. Layne, Carrie, and Simone were already sitting with her, and Amy could guess what they were talking about even without using her incredible auditory skills.

"But Brianna doesn't have any reason to break up with Tuck. They never even fight."

"Maybe she's just bored with him."

"How can she be bored? He's so *cute*!"

"Looks aren't everything. Anyway, I think Billy's cuter than Tuck."

"No way."

"I'll bet you ten Cocodoodles that Brianna and Tuck break up before Friday."

When Amy joined them at the table, she got only the briefest of greetings before the conversation resumed.

"Billy's not just cute, he's got *attitude*. That's why Jenny's so hooked on him."

"I want to know what Danielle's up to. Something's going on in that evil little brain of hers."

"Maybe she's planning to—"

But whatever prediction Layne made was lost in a loud crash. Over by the cafeteria food line, someone had dropped a tray.

This was pretty typical. Almost every day someone dropped a tray, breaking glass and sending food flying. And accidents were always greeted by clapping and cheering and calls to the embarrassed student.

But not today. As Amy gazed around the room, she realized that barely anyone was even glancing in the unfortunate student's direction. They just went right on doing what they were doing. Eating their Cocodoodles, checking out each other's shoelaces, but most of all, talking about *Cherry Lane*.

Clearly, Amy had missed something in her one-and-only viewing of the show. She would definitely give it another chance today.

f4our

When her doorbell rang at five-thirty that afternoon, Amy could practically hear the urgency in the ringing. She ran downstairs and opened the door.

"How was the dentist?" she asked, but Tasha had already pushed past her and was settling herself in front of the TV.

"Did you rewind the tape?" she wanted to know. "Is it ready to watch?"

"No, but it'll only take a second," Amy said. She hit the appropriate button on the remote and the whirring sound indicated that the tape was rewinding. "How did your checkup go?" she asked again. "Do you have any cavities?"

"No," Tasha said. "It went fine." She stared impatiently at the blank TV screen. Amy stared at *her* in bewilderment. Normally Tasha would be regaling her with a detailed description of the horrors she'd encountered in the dentist's office, the physical pain she'd suffered, the emotional agony she'd experienced. Yet here she was, acting like a visit to the dentist was no big deal.

"You want something to eat?" Amy offered. "We've got cheese and onion taco chips."

Those were Tasha's favorite snack. But Tasha was more excited by the fact that the tape had finished rewinding. "C'mon, it's ready!"

Amy settled down next to her with the remote, turned the TV on, and hit Play. The screen was immediately filled with the face of a famous MTV host. "It's a big day on *Total Request Live,* guys and gals! In less than a minute, the Spice Girls reunion will be taking place right here, before your eyes! So don't touch that dial, stay tuned, and we'll be right back!"

"The Spice Girls are having a reunion?" Amy asked. "I didn't even know they ever broke up."

"Where's *Cherry Lane*?" Tasha shrieked.

"Okay, okay, don't get hysterical," Amy said, and she hit the Fast Forward button. A commercial for an acne ointment flew by, followed by commercials for hair gel, sneakers, and a popular boy band's greatest hits. Then five girls in boots and miniskirts jiggled across the screen.

"Amy! Where's *Cherry Lane*?"

Amy had an awful feeling that *Cherry Lane* was nowhere to be found, at least not on this tape. She could see what had happened: The VCR had been set to the wrong channel. Whether this was her fault or a problem with the new remote control, she didn't know, and it didn't matter. The result was the same—Monday's episode of *Cherry Lane* had not been taped.

Tasha looked stricken.

"I'm sorry," Amy said, and she watched in alarm as tears welled up in Tasha's eyes. "Tasha, I'm sorry! It was an accident! Geez, don't cry, it's just a TV show!"

That was clearly the wrong thing to say. In less than a second, Tasha was running out the front door.

Amy raced after her. "Tasha, wait!" She caught up to Tasha and grabbed her arm. Now she could see the tears streaming down her friend's face. "Oh, Tasha, you're really upset!" she cried in wonderment. "Calm down! Take a deep breath! I've never seen you like this before."

With the back of her hand, Tasha wiped her eyes. "I'm okay," she said sniffling. "It was a big disappointment, that's all. I'd been looking forward to it all day."

Amy didn't know what else she could say or do. She stood there awkwardly, an arm around her best friend's shoulder, and felt like she was hugging a total stranger.

A sound from next door caught her attention. She turned to see two girls emerging from Monica's house, and she recognized them both—Simone and Linda, from school. Eagerly she called out to them and waved. She wasn't particularly friendly with either of the girls, but she thought they might distract Tasha.

The two girls crossed the lawn. "Hello," they chorused.

"Hi," Amy said. "What were you doing at Monica's?"

Simone spoke softly. "We were having therapy. There was a sign at school."

"What kind of therapy?" Amy wanted to know. "Are you sick?"

"Monica was treating our fears," Linda said.

Their words grabbed Tasha's attention, and momentarily at least she was pulled out of her misery. "What are you afraid of?"

"I have a fear of flying," Simone said. "And I'm supposed to go on a plane to visit my cousin after school gets out."

"I'm afraid of taking tests," Linda told them. "I panic. And final exams are coming up."

Amy didn't know what surprised her more—the fact that the girls had these fears or the fact that they were admitting the fears to her and Tasha. Both Linda and Simone always tried to come across as cool, and neither of them had ever confided secrets to Amy or Tasha.

But Amy was pleased, since Tasha was taking a real interest in what they were saying. "What did Monica do to you?" Tasha asked.

Linda spoke vaguely. "We looked at colors, and she talked a lot."

Simone was equally vague. "She lit candles. And there was music, I think. Linda, was there music?"

"I can't remember," Linda said. "But I feel so good right now."

"Me too," Simone said dreamily.

Tasha sighed. "*I* don't. I had to go to the dentist and I missed *Cherry Lane*."

"I've got today's episode on tape," Linda said. "Want to come over and watch it? You too, Amy."

Now Amy was truly floored. Linda Riviera had never made any effort to hide her dislike of Amy. And now Linda was inviting her to her home! Could there possibly be any more surprises today?

Needless to say, Tasha was thrilled at the prospect of seeing her favorite show and accepted the invitation immediately. Amy felt like she had no choice but to go along.

Linda didn't live far from the condo community, so the girls walked. Amy had never been to Linda's house before. They weren't just not friends, they didn't even invite each other to big events like birthday parties. Amy had to admit to herself that she was a little curious about seeing the inside of Linda's house and any family members who might be around.

But no one was home, and Linda led them directly to her bedroom, where she had her own TV and VCR. It was a pretty bedroom, all yellow and white, but what drew Amy's eyes was a framed photo on Linda's bureau—a picture of Linda and her best friend, the late Jeanine Bryant. Amy shuddered, remembering the circumstances of Jeanine's death. Jeanine had been Amy's classmate and worst enemy, and for a terrible time, people had thought Amy had something to do with Jeanine's death. Linda had even come right out and called Amy a murderer. She had also accused Amy of trying to kill *her*, too.

And now here Linda was, being Miss Nicey-Nice, passing around a bowl of Cocodoodles and telling everyone to sit down. Linda was better at setting the VCR than Amy had been—she rewound hers, touched the Play button, and immediately they heard the opening music for *Cherry Lane*.

"Do you think anyone in the world is still watching *Sunset*?" Amy wondered out loud. The only response she got was a chorus of "Shhh!" It was just the music, for crying out loud, the show hadn't even started yet! But Amy filled her mouth with Cocodoodles to keep herself from talking and watched the screen.

The opening scene showed Tucker and Billy in tennis clothes, carrying rackets. "Good match," Billy said.

"Yeah, you made a great serve at the end," Tucker said. "Hey, is it true you're taking Leslie Dial to the dance?"

"I asked her. But she already had a date. I don't know who I'll take now."

"How about Jenny?" Tucker suggested.

Billy looked as if Tucker had suggested the Bride of Frankenstein. "Jenny? Why would I ask Jenny? She's just a friend, she's not someone I want to have a date with."

"Isn't there any girl you really like?" Tucker wanted to know.

"Yeah, there's a girl," Billy said.

"Who?"

Billy shrugged. "I don't want to talk about it. Anyway, she's not available."

"Do I know her?" Tucker asked.

Billy turned away from his friend. He gazed off into the distance, and his face took on that sad, faraway look every character on this show seemed to have. "Yes. You know her." Then he turned back with an artificial smile. "C'mon, let's play another set."

The picture dissolved into a commercial, and Tasha let out a squeal. "Ohmigod, Billy likes Brianna!"

Linda spoke in a whisper. "Do you think she knows?"

She was looking at Amy as she spoke, and Amy didn't know what to say. "Can you pass the Cocodoodles, please?" Amy asked. Linda did. Then she picked up the remote and swiftly advanced the tape past the commercial.

In the next scene, Jenny was sitting at a desk, writing. Brianna came into the room. "What are you doing?" Brianna asked.

"I'm writing a letter to Billy," Jenny said. "Listen to this. 'There is someone who loves you very much. Open your eyes and look around.'"

"Oh, Jenny," Brianna sighed. "You're not going to send that letter to him, are you?"

"I won't sign it."

"But he'll know it came from you!"

"Maybe that's a good thing," Jenny said. "I just heard that Leslie Dial is going to the dance with Howie Leake. Maybe this letter will make Billy ask me!"

"Don't send it, Jenny!" Brianna cried out.

"Maybe you're right," Jenny said. "A letter would take too long to get to him. I'll write an e-mail instead."

"Jenny, that's worse!" Brianna made a gesture of despair and closed her eyes. When she opened them, she had that faraway look. The program cut to a commercial.

"She knows Billy is interested in her," Simone said with certainty.

"I'm not so sure about that," Tasha declared. "Maybe *she's* interested in Billy, but she doesn't know how he feels about her."

"You're both wrong," Linda stated. "Brianna wouldn't be interested in Billy when she knows her best friend likes him."

"What's your opinion, Amy?" Simone asked.

Amy had no opinion at all. She didn't even care. And now she was getting that icky feeling in her head again. She took another lemon Cocodoodle and tried to concentrate.

In the next scene, the petite redhead, Danielle, could be seen with an armful of books. She was standing in a hall just outside a classroom door. From the inside of the classroom, Tucker's voice could be heard. "Yes, Mr. Jones, I'll turn in the assignment tomorrow."

Simone gasped. "Good grief, she's *spying* on him!"

"Shhh!" Tasha and Linda hissed.

When Tucker emerged from the class, he didn't see Danielle at first. He started to walk off in the opposite direction. Danielle let the books she was carrying drop to the floor, and he turned around at the sound.

"Hi, Danielle. You need some help with those books?"

"Thank you, Tucker." She let him take all the books, and they walked together down the silent hallway to the exit.

"I've got my car here," Tucker said. "I can give you a ride home."

"That would be great," Danielle said.

They got into Tucker's car. "Where do you live?" he asked.

"Cherry Lane," she replied.

"You're kidding!" he exclaimed. "*I* live on Cherry Lane!"

"I know," Danielle said softly. "I live next door. My family moved in last week."

How dumb could this guy be? Amy thought. He didn't notice a family moving into the house next door?

Tucker laughed. "Well, I guess I won't have any problem finding your house."

"I hope not," Danielle said in a very sexy voice. "Tucker . . . may I ask you a personal question?"

Amy could hear Simone, Linda, and Tasha suck in their collective breath as they waited to hear what Danielle was going to say.

The camera moved in on her face. "It's about Billy," she said.

The scene faded, and the closing music began.

"I can't believe it!" Linda practically screamed. "Now *she* likes Billy!" Tasha and Simone were bouncing up and down in glee.

"This is the best show in the world!" Tasha exclaimed.

Simone agreed. "You never know what's going to happen next!"

Amy said nothing, and her silence must have been conspicuous, because Linda turned to her. "What's the matter, Amy? Don't *you* think it's the best show?"

"Yeah, it's great," Amy said, and gave an excuse for her lack of wild enthusiasm. "I've got a headache, that's all." She was beginning to believe that this strange sensation really was an ordinary headache, the kind other people had. She wondered if the headache could be the result of eating so many Cocodoodles. She didn't usually consume this much sugar.

At least it gave her an excuse to leave. She got up. "Thanks for inviting me, Linda. Tasha, I need to go home."

Normally Tasha would have taken the hint and said "Me too," or something like that. But she was deep in conversation with Simone about the Billy-Brianna-Jenny-Danielle situation.

"Tasha," Amy repeated. "I have to go."

Tasha glanced in her direction. "Okay, see ya."

Walking home alone, Amy couldn't help feeling just a little rejected. And very out of it. Why did they think *Cherry Lane* was so fascinating? It was *boring*. *Sunset* wasn't anything special either, but at least it wasn't dull. Someone was always getting kidnapped, or plotting to kill someone else, or falling down an elevator shaft and waking up with amnesia. On *Cherry Lane*, all the characters did was talk about who liked who.

Amy brightened when she turned her own corner and saw Eric coming out of his house with one of his basketball buddies, Kyle Osborne. They were heading for her front door.

"Hi, guys," she called. "What are you up to?"

"Did you tape today's *Cherry Lane* episode?" Eric asked her.

"I tried to. But the remote messed up. Or maybe I messed up. Anyway, it didn't get taped."

Kyle uttered a curse so strong that Amy was shocked. Kyle didn't usually talk like that, and certainly this circumstance didn't call for such a strong word.

She looked at her watch. "It's a half hour till dinner. You guys want to go skating?"

"No, I want to see that show," Kyle said.

"Me too," Eric echoed. He snapped his fingers. "Hey, I'll bet Spence taped it. Let's call him."

Amy thought she was going to scream. "Can't anyone talk about anything besides *Cherry Lane*?"

Kyle looked at Amy's shoes. "Your shoelaces don't match your shirt."

"There's no law that says they have to match all the time," Amy snapped. She looked at Eric, expecting to see him grin at Kyle's dumb remark. But Eric was looking at his watch.

"C'mon, if I'm going to get back in time for dinner, we gotta start watching now."

"You got any Cocodoodles?" Kyle asked him. "I'm all out."

Amy fished around in her pocket. "Here, you can have mine." She pulled out a pack of grape Cocodoodles, more than half full.

Kyle's eyes narrowed. "How much do you want for them?"

"They're free, Kyle. Just take them."

He stared at her in disbelief. "Are you nuts? Don't you know that half the stores in L.A. are out of these? You could make some serious money. Hey, Morgan, I think your girlfriend's weird."

"Kyle, just take the Cocodoodles and let's go!" Eric was sounding as frantic as Tasha had been earlier. They took off without even saying goodbye, and now it was Amy's turn to stare in disbelief.

And Kyle thought *she* was weird!

f5ve

By the time she arrived home from school the next day, Amy had decided that Tasha, Eric, Simone, Linda, and Kyle weren't the only people acting weird. Stomping through the living room, she glared at the TV. *Cherry Lane* would be coming on in about five minutes, and hers was probably the only TV in a Parkside Middle School home that wouldn't be turned on.

Is the show this popular everywhere or just here? she wondered. She went up to her room, turned on her computer, and accessed a search engine on the Internet. Typing *Cherry Lane* in the correct box, she clicked on Search and waited.

Suddenly the screen was full. At the top, the line read "Page 1 of 50. 4852 responses."

She was stunned. Scrolling down, she speed-read the citations and began clicking at random. Most of the responses took her to personal Web pages, some of which were completely devoted to the show, some even limited to a particular character: "Brianna's Real Story" or "Tucker's Secret," for example. There were photo galleries of the characters, a complete guide to the plot of each episode, and a link to someone selling scripts from the show.

There was a whole category called "Spoilers," where people claimed to know what was going to happen in the future episodes. A *Cherry Lane* line of clothing was being developed, as well as *Cherry Lane* cosmetics and jewelry. There were T-shirts and posters and Cherry Lane street signs for sale, fan clubs to join, and a magazine to subscribe to.

Cherry Lane was taking over the world. Amy felt as if she lived alone on another planet.

Over dinner that evening, she tried to explain her feelings to her mother. "Everyone's getting so obnoxious! All they care about are shoelaces and Cocodoodles and *Cherry Lane*," she said.

Nancy smiled. "I thought you were into shoelaces too."

"Well, sure, I *was*. It used to be fun. But now it's crazy! People actually criticize you if your shoelaces don't match your outfit. Today this girl in my gym class actually accused someone of stealing shoelaces out of her locker! There was a demonstration in the cafeteria, with kids demanding that they start providing Cocodoodles with the school lunches. And I saw a bunch of guys in the hall picking on another guy just because he hasn't been watching *Cherry Lane*."

"*Cherry Lane?*"

"It's a TV show. Everyone's watching it." Amy must have made a face as she spoke, because her mother got the picture.

"Except for you."

Amy nodded. "I can't stand it, it's so dumb. Really, Mom, it's awful. But you should hear the kids at school. They talk about the characters on *Cherry Lane* as if they were real people!"

Nancy laughed. "When I was in college, there was a popular television show called *Dallas*. It was all about these nasty rich folks and their silly love affairs. It was very stupid, but I was just as hooked on it as everyone else. And we used to talk about the characters as if they were real. When the characters had a conflict, people used to take sides and argue about them!"

"It couldn't have been as stupid as *Cherry Lane*," Amy

muttered. "And at least you didn't have Cocodoodles. I am so sick of seeing Cocodoodles, smelling Cocodoodles, listening to everyone chewing on stupid Cocodoodles. Those things don't even taste good. Kids just eat them because everyone else is eating them."

Nancy nodded as if she understood. "That reminds me of Pez."

"Of *what*?"

"Pez. It was a little rectangular candy that came in assorted flavors. We kept them in little plastic containers called Pez dispensers that we would click, and then a Pez would pop out. I had a friend who collected all the different kinds of dispensers." Nancy laughed. "I remember trading a *Partridge Family* Pez dispenser for a *Brady Bunch* one."

Amy stared at her mother, the university professor, the biological scientist. "You're kidding," she said flatly.

"No, I'm not kidding," her mother replied. "My point is, fads like TV shows and candies are not so unusual."

"But Cocodoodles and *Cherry Lane* are stupid!"

"Most fads are pretty silly," Nancy said. "Really, Amy, you shouldn't be so judgmental. It's perfectly normal for kids your age to get into silly trends. They don't last forever. I don't see what the problem is, as long as the trends aren't dangerous or unhealthy."

"Those Cocodoodles can't be very healthy," Amy grumbled. "They're giving me headaches."

She thought that remark would force her mother to take this more seriously. Instead, Nancy just smiled. "I'm sure that's just psychosomatic, Amy."

Amy didn't like the sound of that. "Are you saying I'm nuts?"

"No, honey, you're not nuts. You're just having an emotional reaction. You're feeling frustrated, so you're giving yourself headaches."

Amy was definitely frustrated, and her mother's words were making her feel even more so. "Then you think this is okay, the way kids are acting?"

"I'm just saying it's normal, Amy." At least now her mother was looking more sympathetic. "I can see why this is hard for you to understand."

"Because I'm not normal?"

"Well, in a way, yes. You're more intelligent, more mature than other kids your age. You can't be as easily amused or entertained."

Amy couldn't buy that. In the past, she and Tasha had enjoyed lots of the same activities. Why should things become different now? Because she was getting older? Would she continue to mature faster than everyone else?

The notion didn't exactly fill her with pleasure. If she

was going to become even more different from everyone else, who was she going to hang out with? A future of isolation and loneliness hovered before her eyes.

Depression must have been written all over her face. "Amy, it's not the end of the world," Nancy chided her. "Just don't be so hard on your friends. Keep an open mind; try to understand why everyone's so excited about these things."

Amy scowled. "You want me to eat Cocodoodles and pretend I like this dumb TV show?"

Now her mother was beginning to look irritated. "Amy, this will pass. A month from now, the kids will be watching a different TV show and eating a different candy. I don't understand why you're making such a big deal about this. Either you get into the fad or you ignore it and wait for it to be over. But don't turn it into a crisis!"

Just then they heard someone pounding on the front door. Nancy opened it to Monica, who looked flustered and nervous.

"Nancy, by any remote possibility, do you have any vanilla-scented candles? Or incense?"

Since this was Monica speaking, Nancy didn't seem particularly surprised by the odd request. "No, I don't think so. What's the matter?"

"I've got a patient coming in fifteen minutes who

says she hasn't slept well in days," Monica told her. "I have a terrific treatment for her, but it calls for vanilla aroma and I'm all out of candles and incense. And the stores are closed. I don't know what to do!"

Nancy considered the problem. "Well, if it's the scent of vanilla that you need, why not just use real vanilla extract?"

"Huh?"

"I think I have some in the kitchen," Nancy said, and went back there.

"Are you getting lots of patients?" Amy asked Monica.

Monica nodded happily. "It's going well, I think. And I owe you a great big thank-you, Amy. That sign you put up at your school has really attracted some attention! I've treated four Parkside students, and a dozen more have made appointments. It seems like a lot of your friends are feeling stressed out lately."

"Classmates, not friends," Amy muttered glumly. "I have no friends."

Nancy returned with a little bottle. "Here, Monica. Just wave this in front of your patients' noses. They'll get a real whiff of vanilla."

"Nancy, you're brilliant! Thank you so much." Monica turned back to Amy. "I guess you must be excited about the special show Thursday evening. Your classmates who came to see me today talked my ear off about it."

"What special show?" Nancy asked.

Amy knew what Monica was talking about. There was no way she couldn't, since it had been the hot topic of conversation all day. "There's going to be a special one-hour prime-time episode of *Cherry Lane*."

Her mother looked thoughtful. And later, after Monica had left, she made a proposal. "Amy, would you like to invite some friends over to watch the special show on Thursday night?"

Amy was appalled. "Why would I want to do something like that?"

"So you won't feel so left out. Now, I'm not saying you have to go along with this fad just because everyone else is into it. But you know it's not good for you to stand out, to seem too different from everyone else."

Amy hated to admit it, but her mother was making a good point. Amy knew she wasn't supposed to draw too much attention to herself. And if she was the only kid at Parkside who wasn't watching *Cherry Lane*, she would definitely be considered different.

"You could turn this into a little party," her mother urged. "We'll get snacks and sodas and order pizzas. Is there anything special I should get?"

Amy sighed. "Better stock up on Cocodoodles."

six

"I can invite ten people," Amy told Tasha and Eric on the way to school Wednesday. "You guys, of course. Carrie and Layne. Maybe Tiffany from phys ed. Do you think I should ask Simone and Linda? I watched the show at Linda's on Monday, so it would be the nice thing to do, I guess. But we're not really friends. What do you think, Tasha? Should I invite them?"

"Yes," Tasha said.

Amy turned to Eric. "I should invite some other guys, too, so you won't be the only one. Do you think Kyle would want to come?"

"He can't come," Eric said. "Neither can I. We have a basketball game tomorrow night."

Amy clapped a hand to her mouth. "Oh no, Eric, I forgot! I was planning to go to that one!"

"It's okay," Eric said mildly.

He was being so understanding. Usually he got annoyed when she couldn't come to a big game. "I'll tape the *Cherry Lane* special for you," she offered.

"Thanks," he said.

She turned back to Tasha. "Well, if Eric can't come, I could make it just girls. What do you think? Just girls, or girls and guys?"

Tasha smiled. "I don't care. Either way is fine with me."

Amy was startled. Tasha always had an opinion, and she never hesitated to express it.

Amy was trying very hard to get into the whole *Cherry Lane* party thing. She knew she had to fake some enthusiasm if she was going to get anyone to come. People were so serious about this show, she had to act like she was taking it seriously too.

But she was pleasantly surprised by the reaction to her invitations. Everyone she invited accepted, and Linda Riviera was particularly nice. "Why, thank you, Amy. I would love to come."

Amy tried to remember whether Linda had ever

smiled at her before. "And bring any shoelaces you want to trade," she added.

"Okay," Linda said, still smiling.

Lots of people seemed to be smiling that day. Or at least they weren't as aggressive as usual. In between classes, when kids crowded in the halls, no one pushed and shoved. Everyone seemed more relaxed and in less of a hurry.

Amy mentioned this to Tasha and the others sitting with them at lunch. "Do you think it's the weather?" she asked. "It hasn't rained in ages. Or maybe it's because the school year's almost over."

But no one offered any clue as to why people were so easygoing. They just nodded and agreed that the students seemed to be in generally good moods, and went back to discussing the plights of the residents of *Cherry Lane*.

Others noticed the pleasant atmosphere. In French class, Madame Duquesne complimented them, in French of course. *"Je suis contente, mes enfants! Vous êtes très gentils, et si polis aujourd'hui!"*

Amy agreed. People seemed kinder *and* better-behaved. Dr. Noble even called for their attention over the intercom during the last period. "Boys and girls, I have a very exciting announcement to make. Today, for the first time since I have been the principal at

Parkside Middle School, hall monitors have reported *no infractions!*"

Is this a new fad, Amy wondered? Has there ever been such a thing as a behavior fad? She doubted it would last as long as shoelaces.

But the pleasant behavior was still in effect on Thursday. It even seemed to have spread. During second period, there was a fire drill, which was always an excuse for students to act goofy. But this time students stayed in their lines when they were marched outside. And once outside, they remained pretty quiet. Even Alan Greenfield didn't make any stupid jokes about seeing smoke and sparks.

What was even more amazing was the fact that the ordinary chaos that ruled in the cafeteria at lunchtime had almost completely disappeared. "It's so calm in here," Amy marveled. But no one at the table responded. They continued to talk quietly about *Cherry Lane*.

Amy tried to follow what they were saying. She'd watched the show for the past couple of days, and as far as she could tell, nothing much had happened. When there was a break in the conversation, she broke in, to show them all that she had been keeping up. "Billy got the e-mail from Jenny yesterday, didn't he? Then, at the end of the show, he was looking up Jenny's number in the phone book, right?"

The others looked at her kindly, as if she was a very young and not very bright child who had just learned a new word. "Yes, that's right, Amy," Layne said. "We know that Billy is about to *call* Jenny. But we don't know what Billy will *say* to Jenny."

"We'll probably find out tonight," Carrie said.

"At my house," Amy reminded them. "Don't forget!"

"We won't," they chorused.

Walking home that afternoon with Tasha, Amy expressed her anxiety about the party. "I want everything to be perfect," she said. "It's weird, I've been feeling sort of out of touch with everyone, and I think it has something to do with not being into the show. So I'm really trying to figure out why everyone likes it so much. And it's not just because I don't want people to think I'm different. I really don't like feeling left out, you know what I mean?"

Tasha didn't respond. Amy realized that her friend had been almost completely silent all the time they'd been walking. "Tasha? Is something wrong?"

Tasha smiled at her. "Everything's fine, Amy."

"You're so quiet today," Amy commented. "Do you feel okay?"

"I feel very good," Tasha said.

"You're certainly very relaxed," Amy remarked. "Did you have one of Monica's therapies?"

"No, I didn't," Tasha said.

She certainly didn't sound sick. But she didn't sound like herself. Still, Amy couldn't worry about that now. The party was giving her more than enough to worry about. "I hope everything goes okay tonight."

"Everything will be fine," Tasha said.

At quarter to seven that evening, Amy surveyed the living room. Everything seemed to be in place. The furniture had been pushed around so that everyone would be able to see the TV, and pillows had been piled on the floor for those who wanted to get really close to the screen. Big bowls of Cocodoodles in every flavor had been strategically placed around the room so no one would have to reach too far to get them. There were sodas in the refrigerator, and the pizzas had arrived. Amy's mother would reheat them and present them during a commercial break.

Nancy was in the kitchen with Tasha's mother, who had brought over one of her famous cheesecakes for the party. Amy went in there now to get bowls of nuts and popcorn, just in case anyone besides her was sick of Cocodoodles.

"What do you know about this PC program?" Mrs. Morgan was asking Amy's mother.

"It's some new educational philosophy," Nancy said. "The basic idea is to ignore small behavioral problems among kids and concentrate on the big problems. The Positive Control group believes that if you ban weapons and drugs from schools, and if you also ban, say, baseball caps, you trivialize the weapons and drugs by making them equal to baseball caps."

"Do you agree?"

"I don't know," Nancy said. "I suppose it's a worthwhile approach. Amy, have you noticed any improvements at school since they instituted this PC policy?"

"Kids aren't as noisy," Amy told her. "They're more polite. And they're smiling a lot."

"Well, that's definitely an improvement," Mrs. Morgan commented. "Have fun tonight." She was halfway out the door when Nancy poked Amy.

"Don't you have something to say to Mrs. Morgan?"

"Huh?"

"Amy!" Her mother looked pointedly at the cheesecake.

"Oh, right." Amy ran to the door and yelled, "Thank you for the cheesecake, Mrs. Morgan!"

Nancy frowned. "That PC philosophy doesn't seem to be having much effect on *your* manners."

Amy didn't answer. She knew she was forgetting something, and she had to think. Fortunately, her excellent memory didn't let her down.

"Mom, I have to tape the show for Eric. Could you

set the timer for me? That new remote control you bought is weird."

She ran upstairs to get her collection of shoelaces. When she came back down, her mother was still standing in front of the TV with the remote control, and she was frowning.

"I thought this thing was supposed to simplify my life," she grumbled. "There, that should do it."

Finally everything was ready, and just in time. At precisely seven o'clock, Layne and Carrie arrived, followed immediately by Tasha. By 7:02 all the girls Amy invited had arrived. Amy had planned to have a shoelaces trade first, and she had thought of a way to trade them that would break the ice and create a party atmosphere.

"Let's throw all our shoelaces in a pile in the middle of the floor," she suggested. "At the signal, everyone has to dive in and grab the ones they want. Only you can't take any more than you put in. Okay?" She imagined girls grabbing the two ends of the same shoelace and giggling as they battled for it.

No one seemed particularly excited by the idea, but no one complained, either, so Amy collected the laces everyone had brought and put them in the center of the living room floor. "Now, form a circle around the pile of laces," she instructed them. Obediently they followed her instructions.

Her mother had come into the room just in time to hear the plan, and she didn't look very pleased with it. Amy figured she was concerned that things would get broken in the wild scramble.

As it turned out, her mother had nothing to worry about. Amy gave the signal, but none of the girls rushed forward to retrieve the laces they wanted. Carrie, Layne, and Linda went to the pile and quietly selected a few. The others didn't even bother. They'd started sucking on the Cocodoodles and guessing about what would happen on *Cherry Lane* that evening. Amy decided that the shoelace fad had run out of steam, and she wondered which would go next, the Cocodoodles or *Cherry Lane*.

At least Amy didn't have to worry about entertaining her guests for the rest of the hour until the show came on. They were all perfectly content to sit quietly, chew on their Cocodoodles, and make their predictions. They talked about something else, too.

"I saw Monica Jackson for a treatment yesterday," Layne was telling the group. "And today I scored more points than anyone in volleyball."

Amy wasn't sure she got the connection. "What kind of treatment did you have, Layne?"

"It was the energizing therapy," Layne said. "Mostly aroma, but some hypnosis, too."

"You were hypnotized?" another girl asked. "Was it scary?"

"Not at all," Layne said. "It was like going to sleep and being awake at the same time. And it worked! Ms. Talley in phys ed used to say I was the laziest player in class. Well, not anymore!"

Simone had a story about a Monica Jackson treatment too. "I was hypnotized today, for my fear of flying. And I know I could get on a plane right this minute and I wouldn't panic at all."

"Does she have any love potions?" Carrie asked. "I've got such a crush on Cliff Fields."

"I don't think she does any kind of magic," Layne said. "But maybe she could give you a treatment for confidence, and then you'd have the guts to flirt with him."

Amy wondered if Monica's treatments were going to replace shoelaces as the next big fad. At least it gave the group a topic besides *Cherry Lane* to talk about. But by five minutes to eight, everyone was urging Amy to turn on the TV, just in case their watches were slow.

This meant they had to sit through half a dozen commercials, including one for the show itself. "Coming up next—one full hour of *Cherry Lane!*" the announcer intoned.

"You know, it's not really an hour," Amy commented.

"If you take out the commercials, it's probably something like forty-seven minutes."

"Shhh," several people said. And the program hadn't even started!

Finally the familiar music that introduced the show began. Since this was a special, the opening music and scenes of the characters went on longer than usual, but no one said a word. They didn't even speak during the commercials that followed the opening.

The actual show began with a scene in what appeared to be Jenny's bedroom. Jenny was brushing her hair, looking very happy for a change. There was a knock on her door. "Come in," she called out.

Brianna entered. "Hi, I'm going to the mall. Want to come?"

"I can't," Jenny said. "I'm meeting Billy at the coffee shop!"

Brianna looked startled. "You are?"

"I sent him the e-mail, and he just called. He wants to talk!" Jenny hugged herself. "Oh, Brianna, I'm so happy. Now he knows how I feel about him, and he feels the same way about me!"

"Did he tell you that?" Brianna asked.

"Well, no. But he said he wants to talk to me about something very important. What else can it be? I'm sure he's going to say he loves me."

"Oh, Jenny, how can you be so sure?" Brianna asked.

"Brianna, for every girl in the world, there is one boy. It doesn't matter if he's in China and she's in Texas. If it's true love, they will find each other. I'm just very lucky that my one true love lives on my street."

Amy wanted to gag. The rest of the scene consisted of Jenny trying to decide what to wear for the meeting and Brianna gazing off into the distance with a faraway expression.

At the commercial break, the scene was analyzed. "Maybe it will be okay," Tiffany said. "After all, we don't really know how Billy feels, do we?"

"He told Tuck he thinks of Jenny as a friend, that's all," Linda reminded her.

"But he could have changed his mind after reading her e-mail," Layne suggested optimistically.

They didn't find out in the next scene. This one focused on Brianna and Tuck. It began with Brianna leaving Jenny's house and seeing a light on across the street in Tuck's bedroom. She knocked on the door and Tuck let her in.

Amy had a pretty good idea what was going to happen. Tuck was talking about how he had to study for a big geography test, and Brianna kept doing her faraway looks, making it clear she wasn't listening. Then it came—the big breakup scene. Brianna told Tuck she loved him as a friend but she didn't think they were meant to be together.

"You see, Tuck, for every girl in the world, there is one boy. And for every boy, there is one girl. I am not your girl, and you are not my boy."

It was getting harder for Amy to resist making the gagging noise. This was too corny for words. Plus she was getting that headachy feeling again.

"Have you found your boy?" Tucker asked.

With her faraway look, Brianna answered, "Yes, I think I have." The music swelled and the scene dissolved into a commercial.

"Time for pizza!" Amy announced happily.

Nobody got excited. Amy's mother brought out the pizzas, but the girls barely glanced at them. Some of them were acting like they were on the verge of tears.

"It's Billy she loves, I knew it all along," Simone said.

"But Jenny's her best friend!" Tasha cried out. "How can she do that to her?"

"I feel so sorry for Tucker," Layne murmured.

"Who wants pepperoni?" Amy asked. But no one seemed to care what kind of pizza they ate.

In the next scene, at the coffee shop, Billy told Jenny he wasn't interested in her as a girlfriend. Jenny ran out crying and ran into Tuck—or rather, he almost ran into her, literally. He was driving around aimlessly and nearly hit her with his car. They went off together to console each other, just missing Brianna, who came looking for Billy. As they sat together and talked, Danielle came in and gave Brianna a nasty look. Just as Brianna was about to tell him she loved him, Billy got a call on his mobile phone. His evil identical twin brother, Mitchell, had just escaped from reform school. Billy left the coffee shop. Commercial.

Amy couldn't believe there was an evil identical twin. How dumb could this show get?

Even dumber. In the final scene, Danielle was driving down a highway. She spotted a hitchhiker who looked just like Billy, and she stopped to pick him up. Only it wasn't Billy, it was Mitchell. It turned out that this meeting was all planned, that Danielle used to be at the reform school too, and that they had this elaborate scheme to mess up the lives of everyone who lived on Cherry Lane.

When the show ended, there was dead silence in Amy's living room.

"Anyone want some ice cream?" Amy asked, without much hope. She could see that no one was interested in eating. Most of her guests had a glazed-over expression, like they were still in a state of shock at the turn of events.

There was a soft chorus of thank-yous as they all

began to leave. Amy stopped Tasha at the door. "Do you have to go right now? Can't you stick around for a while?"

Tasha smiled, but she shook her head, and her expression was very much like Brianna's, all dreamy and faraway. "Thank you, Amy," she murmured, and floated out with the rest of them.

Amy's mother came into the room and looked around in satisfaction. "Well, your friends certainly didn't make much of a mess," she said happily.

Amy thought about the way most rooms looked after a party. This didn't look right. But then again, at most parties people didn't spend the entire time sitting still, glued to a TV set.

Minutes later, Eric returned from his basketball game. Amy opened the door and invited him in. "How was the game?" she asked.

"Fine," he said.

"What was the score?"

"Forty-four to six."

"Wow!" Amy exclaimed. "You really clobbered them!"

"No," Eric said. "They clobbered us." But he didn't seem at all upset by this.

"Want some pizza?" Amy asked him. "There's plenty left."

"No, thank you," Eric said. "Are there any Cocodoodles?"

Amy looked around. The bowls that had held the Cocodoodles were empty. "How about nuts and popcorn?" she offered, but Eric wasn't interested.

"Then I'll rewind the tape for you," Amy said. "You can take it home with you."

"Our VCR is broken," Eric said.

"Oh yeah, I forgot. Well, you can watch it here if you want."

But it turned out that her mother had been no better at figuring out the new remote control than she had been. The *Cherry Lane* special had not been taped.

Eric wasn't upset. "That's okay," he said. "I'll get it from someone else." He started back toward the door.

Amy followed him. "Eric, do you want to go skating after school tomorrow?"

"I'm sorry, I can't," he said. "I have basketball practice."

"Oh. Well, we can go this weekend. By the way, have you found any secondhand skates?"

"What?"

"Eric! I gave you my money, remember? You're supposed to be looking for in-line skates to buy for us."

He nodded. "Yes, I remember. No, I haven't found any yet."

Amy's mother came in. "Hi, Eric. Want some pizza?"

"No, thank you, Ms. Candler," Eric said.

"A soda? Popcorn?"

"No, thank you," Eric said again. "But it was very nice of you to offer. Goodbye, Amy, see you tomorrow."

"See you," Amy echoed.

"Well, Eric's manners have certainly improved," Nancy remarked after he'd left.

Amy nodded. "Yes, they certainly have." In fact, she'd never seen Eric behave so politely before. One more strange occurrence in a week that had been full of them.

Now Amy was getting nervous.

seven
7

By Monday morning, four days after her party, Amy was no longer nervous. Now she was downright scared.

Lying in bed, staring up at the ceiling, she hit the rewind on her mental VCR and considered the past few days. There was the incident on Friday morning, when Tasha and Eric arrived at her door for the walk to school. They were early—*that* was strange. But their reasons were stranger still.

"I want to go to the school library and do research for my sociology term paper," Eric told her.

"I'm planning to clean out my locker before home-room," Tasha said.

Amy's eyes darted back and forth between them. "This is a joke, right?"

"No, it's not a joke," Eric said. "I want to raise my grade in sociology."

"And I'm trying to become better organized," Tasha declared. "After your party last week, I spent two hours cleaning out my closet and organizing my dresser drawers." She spoke with pride, as if she expected Amy to compliment her on her accomplishment.

"Are you ready to leave?" Eric asked.

"No, I haven't had any breakfast yet," Amy replied. "Come on in and have something to eat with us."

"No, thank you," Tasha and Eric said in unison.

"Mom's heating up cinnamon rolls," Amy wheedled. But that didn't tempt them.

"We want to get to school early," Eric explained.

"I'll see you at lunch, Amy," Tasha added.

Dumbfounded, Amy returned to the breakfast table and reported the bizarre conversation to her mother. Nancy didn't think it was so strange.

"It sounds to me like they're trying to make some positive changes in their habits. I think that's excellent. What's wrong with wanting to improve your grades and organize your life?"

Amy had no answer, but she disagreed with her mother. Something was definitely wrong.

And whatever was happening to her friends, it was spreading. When she walked into her homeroom, she thought for a second that everyone was sleeping in their seats. But their eyes were open and directed toward the books that were open on their desks. *Books*—real textbooks and library books. Not comics or magazines. And there was total silence, except for the occasional chewing and sucking sounds that indicated the constant presence of Cocodoodles.

When Ms. Weller came in, she beamed at them. "I don't know what you folks are up to, but whatever it is, keep it up!" Once again, there were no tardy students and no absences. At the end of the morning announcements, an ecstatic Dr. Noble came on the intercom to tell the school that for the first time in three years, one hundred percent of the student body had on-time attendance.

In every one of Amy's classes that morning, the students were in their seats when the bell rang. No one was whispering to a neighbor or passing notes or looking out a window. When teachers asked questions, hands went up and answers were given. Of course, the answers weren't always correct.

Amy was actually relieved in English when Dwayne

Hicks said that Tom Sawyer was the author of *The Adventures of Huckleberry Finn*. At least he was exhibiting normal behavior. But when no one laughed at his response or even teased him about it, she began to think her classmates' bodies had been taken over by well-behaved aliens.

A real shock awaited her in the cafeteria at lunch, and this time it wasn't the lack of commotion or the soft hum of conversation. When she reached her usual table, where Tasha, Layne, and Carrie were sitting, she saw that the day's lunch included the infamous mystery meat. *That* wasn't unusual; Mystery Meat appeared at least twice a month. What was absolutely, utterly unbelievable was the fact that everyone was *eating* it.

Amy couldn't remember ever seeing anyone eat the brown stuff before. All sorts of jokes were made about it, and it was the main weapon in any food fight. But no one ever ate it. Until today.

"Why are you eating the mystery meat?" she managed to ask.

Tasha and the others all looked at her as if she was crazy. "Because that's what we're having for lunch," Tasha said.

"It must be good for us, or the school wouldn't want us to eat it," Layne said.

"We should be grateful to have such nutritious food," Carrie added.

Amy backed away.

"Where are you going?" Tasha asked.

"I—I have to go to the library," Amy said, and fled the cafeteria.

It was like that all day. Kids were quiet, polite, and agreeable, and they did everything they were supposed to do. There was no running in the halls, no slamming of locker doors, no fights, no tears, no name-calling. At the end of the day, just before the bell, Dr. Noble came on the intercom to announce that for the first time *ever* in the entire history of Parkside Middle School, no one had detention.

"Amy! Breakfast!"

Now, on Monday morning, her mother's voice brought her back to the present. She dragged herself out of bed, washed, brushed, and dressed, and went downstairs. Her mother looked at her reprovingly.

"Tasha and Eric have already come and gone," she told her.

"Did you notice anything different about them?" Amy asked hopefully.

"Different in what way?"

What could Amy say now? *Did they resemble zombies?* "Nothing," she said. She gulped down some juice, grabbed a slice of toast, and took off. She was supposed to get to school early today too, for a student council meeting.

The meeting began normally, which meant it was just as boring as usual, with the call to order and the reading of the minutes of the last meeting. But this time, Amy observed that no one was fidgeting. None of them had their eyes closed; no one was even yawning. The council members stared at the front of the room. They were attentive and actually listening to the secretary read the minutes from the last boring meeting. Amy's thoughts drifted back to the day before, at the Sunshine Square parking lot.

She'd gone by herself. Eric was studying, Mrs. Morgan had told her happily, and didn't want to go skating. There were other kids on the lot, skating and boarding, but it was all quieter than usual. Amy had skated around in circles, trying to organize her thoughts and come to some conclusion about what was going on, when suddenly a skateboarder collided with an in-line skater.

They ran smack into each other, and both were knocked to the ground. Amy watched nervously. Neither of the boys appeared to be injured, but this was just the kind of incident that could create a huge fight between the opposing groups.

The skateboarder got up first. He gave the in-line skater a hand to help him up. "I'm sorry," the skateboarder said.

"That's all right, it was my fault," the in-line skater replied. After exchanging bland smiles, they took off in opposite directions.

Remembering the incident, Amy shuddered. This couldn't be simply a behavior trend, a courtesy fad. This was a disease, an infection, something strange and profound and truly scary.

Now, at the meeting, Cliff Fields droned on and on as he asked for a motion to approve the minutes, then called for a second to the motion, then called for a vote on the motion. "All in favor of approving the minutes, blah, blah, blah." At this point in the meeting there should have been audible groans.

But with the exception of Cliff Fields, the room was silent. The kids continued to look straight ahead, with vacant expressions and a few bland smiles. It was eerie. Amy had a sudden image of a Halloween sleepover party last year, when the guests had watched old horror movies from the 1950s and 1960s. *Invasion of the Body Snatchers. Night of the Living Dead.*

She raised her hand.

"The president recognizes Amy Candler," Cliff said.

Amy rose from her chair. "Um . . . I was just wondering if anyone else has noticed something kind of weird going on. . . ."

Just like her mother, Cliff asked, "In what way?"

This was where Amy really had to struggle for words. "Everyone's acting different, like, like . . . well, not like themselves!" She looked around the room. "Even here, you're all acting so out of it!"

Cliff popped a Cocodoodle in his mouth. "I don't understand, Amy. What do you mean, out of it?"

"Too quiet, and nice, and stiff, and polite!" Even as the words came out of her mouth, she could hear how ridiculous she sounded.

Carrie raised her hand. "Being nice and quiet and polite are *good* things, Amy. Not weird."

"Is there any more new business?" Cliff asked the group.

A boy rose. "I'm starting a petition to ask the company that makes Cocodoodles to make cherry-flavored ones. In honor of *Cherry Lane*."

"Excellent idea," Cliff said.

Carrie's hand went up again. "*I've* got an announcement about *Cherry Lane* too. You've all probably heard that a *Cherry Lane* movie is being made. The company that made the movie is going to choose a school to host the premiere. I want to start a campaign to get the movie shown here, at Parkside."

"Another excellent idea," Cliff said. "Is there any more new business? No? Is there a motion to adjourn?"

As soon as the meeting was over, Amy hurried to Carrie's side. "Carrie, I didn't mean that it's wrong to be polite. But don't you think people are kind of over-doing it?"

"Calm down, Amy," Carrie said. "Here, have a Cocodoodle."

Amy looked at the little candy that Carrie gave her. She shoved it into her pocket and ran out the door. Now what? Someone *had* to listen to her!

She still had a few minutes before homeroom. She ran to the principal's office and asked the secretary if she could see Dr. Noble.

"They're having a faculty meeting across the hall in the teachers' lounge," the secretary told her. "You'll have to wait."

But Amy was in no mood to wait. She went out into the hall and was about to knock on the lounge door when she realized that the voices inside sounded ex-cited. Maybe they'd already figured out that something peculiar had happened to the students. She listened.

A teacher was speaking. "It's incredible! They're

showing up in class, they're listening, they're doing their homework assignments—what's going on?"

Others chimed in. "I didn't have to reprimand one student in the cafeteria last week."

"And they're putting all their trash in the appropriate recycling bins!"

"The custodian told me that there's no new graffiti in the boys' bathroom."

"It's almost scary!" another teacher said.

Exactly, Amy thought, and she started to feel hopeful. But her hopes were dashed when she heard a third voice declare, "Scary and *fabulous!*" And a chorus of voices echoed the feeling, with cries of "Yes!"

She heard Dr. Noble say, "Our mission now is to keep them on this track. And I believe that if we continue to follow the guidelines set forth by Positive Control, things can only get better and better. I predict that in the future, we will have no need to schedule any of you to serve as monitors in detention!"

That announcement drew actual cheers. And Amy realized that there was no point in knocking at the door. She should have guessed that teachers would prefer obedient robots to normal, noisy, annoying, misbehaving kids.

She looked at the clock on the wall. The bell would

ring in precisely fifty seconds. Right now the halls of Parkside Middle School should be ringing with yelling and running and lockers slamming. But the halls were silent. The students were already in their homerooms, in their seats, quiet and attentive. Silent. Except for the crunching and chewing of Cocodoodles.

Amy felt in her pocket for the Cocodoodle Carrie had given her. Then she took out the little yellow ball and studied it. Could there be something in this innocent-looking candy that was affecting them all?

Her heartbeat quickened at the thought. It would explain a lot if these candies contained some drug, some chemical, that was turning her classmates into zombies. Amy hadn't reacted to them, but that made sense—she had a different genetic structure than others. And that could explain why she had been getting headaches; maybe that was her special body's unique response to the chemical.

She ducked into the girls' rest room for a piece of toilet paper to wrap the candy so that it would be carefully preserved. Then she went to homeroom, barely making it on time. And she didn't miss the stern looks some of her classmates gave her. She'd almost spoiled their one hundred percent on-time attendance record.

Somehow she made it through another very strange

day of perfect students. She didn't bother trying to question Tasha and the others at lunch, and she didn't attempt to bring the odd behavior to anyone's attention. If her suspicions were correct, the answer might lie in a piece of candy.

As soon as school let out, she left the building and took a bus to downtown Los Angeles. She made her way to Westside Hospital and went to the reception desk. "Could you page Dr. David Hopkins, please?"

She had to thumb through about five old magazines before Dr. Dave finally appeared in the lobby. He was alarmed when he saw Amy.

"Amy, are you all right?"

"I'm fine," Amy assured him. "But a lot of kids at my school are *not*. They've been acting strange, like, I don't know how to explain it, but it's weird, I mean—"

Dr. Dave interrupted her. "Amy, I'm awfully busy right now. The victims of a ten-car collision are on their way to the emergency room. What do you need?"

Amy took the wrapped Cocodoodle from her pocket. "Could you get this checked for drugs?"

"What kind of drugs?" Dr. Dave asked.

"I don't know. Mind-altering drugs." She thought of the ones she'd heard about. "LSD, angel dust, Ecstasy, that kind of thing."

A sharp voice called out from a loudspeaker somewhere. "Dr. Hopkins, code blue. Dr. Hopkins, code blue."

"I have to go, Amy," Dr. Dave said hurriedly. He took the Cocodoodle from her and dropped it into his lab coat pocket. "I'll see what I can do."

Coming home, Amy was in much better spirits. She really believed that the candy could be the answer to the nightmare that was unfolding before her eyes. Dr. Dave would identify the evil chemical, the Cocodoodle Candy Company would immediately respond by taking all the products off the shelves, and people would go back to being normal.

As she approached her own door, she saw a man getting out of a truck. He was carrying a large box, which he brought to the Morgan house.

Amy watched as Eric opened the door and accepted the box. Amy strolled over. "What's that?" she asked as Eric signed a paper and the man went back to his truck.

"A new VCR." Eric gave her that vacant smile he'd been smiling lately.

"Great," she said. "You finally talked your parents into it, huh?"

"No," he said. "They wouldn't buy one for us. So I used my own money."

"Your own money?" Amy frowned. "You mean the money you were saving for skates?"

"Yes."

Amy thought of something else. "A VCR costs more money than you had. Eric, did you use *my* money too?"

"Yes," he said pleasantly. "I did. I knew you wouldn't mind. After all, *Cherry Lane* is a lot more important than skating. Don't you think so? Amy? Amy, why are you looking at me like that?"

Amy knew that in his current condition he wouldn't understand. So she just turned away and went home.

e8ght

"**W**ould you like to sign the petition for cherry-flavored Cocodoodles?" an eighth-grade boy asked Amy the next day in the cafeteria.

"No," Amy said.

The eighth grader looked at her as if she'd been speaking a foreign language. "No?"

Amy rolled her eyes. "No, thank you."

Before she made it to her seat, three more students asked if she would sign a petition for cherry Cocodoodles. When the fourth kid asked, she almost lost her temper.

"I'm *not* going to sign any petition for Cocodoodles,

cherry or blueberry or any other flavor! I don't even *like* Cocodoodles!"

That particular girl gasped. "You don't like Cocodoodles?"

By the time Amy made it to her table, she had a feeling that the entire cafeteria was staring at her. She would now be known forever as the girl who didn't like Cocodoodles.

No sooner had she sat down than Layne turned to her with that horrible vacant smile. "Hi, Amy! Would you sign my petition for—"

Amy wanted to scream. "I'm not signing any petition for Cocodoodles!"

"But this isn't for Cocodoodles, Amy," Layne said. "It's a petition to get the *Cherry Lane* movie premiere here at Parkside."

"Oh." But that idea wasn't any more appealing than cherry Cocodoodles. "Actually, Layne, it wouldn't be honest for me to sign it. See . . . I don't watch *Cherry Lane* every day. I don't really like it."

Her voice must have carried. People from the tables around them were staring at her in utter disbelief. Some of them even looked frightened, as if Amy was some sort of monster alien that had wandered into their midst.

She got up. "Excuse me," she said, and walked out,

but she could feel eyes following her. Thank goodness she had a granola bar in her bag. She'd have to find a quiet, unoccupied corner and eat alone. She made a mental note to tell her mother to stock up on granola bars. Amy had a feeling she'd be eating a lot of lunches alone.

Unless, maybe, Dr. Dave came through for her with some interesting news.

She didn't dare go back to the hospital after school and disturb him again. He'd tell her mother and her mother would lecture her. She'd just have to be patient and hope that he wouldn't forget and would get the candy tested soon.

She was so anxious about this that she even thought of asking Monica for one of her relaxation treatments. Passing Monica's house that afternoon on her way home, she could see through the window that half a dozen kids were sitting in the living room, which Monica now referred to as the waiting room. Amy recognized most of the kids as students at Parkside. And in the time it took to cover the short distance between Monica's house and her own, two more Parkside kids arrived. Clearly, Monica was a hit with the young teen crowd.

Inside her own house, Amy moved around restlessly. She wasn't hungry, and she wasn't in the mood to get her homework done. She was feeling so hyped up, she almost considered watching *Cherry Lane* at four-thirty— but that would only make her think about cherry Cocodoodles.

Just before five, the phone rang. Amy answered it. "Hello?"

"Hi, Amy, how are you?"

"Dr. Dave, hi!"

"Is your mother there?"

"No, this is Tuesday, she has an evening class to teach."

"Oh, right. Well, just tell her I called, okay? See you."

"Dr. Dave, wait!" She shouldn't bug him, but she couldn't help it. "Did you find out anything about the Cocodoodle?"

"The *what*?"

"The candy I gave you to test for drugs!"

"Oh, that. Yes, I had the candy put through all the standard tests. It's just candy, Amy, that's all. It's full of artificial flavors and junk like that, but it's completely harmless."

"Oh." Disappointment crashed down on her like a brick.

He must have been able to hear it in her voice. "Why did you think there were drugs in the candy?"

"Because the kids at my school are eating them all the time, and they've been acting weird."

He spoke kindly. "You know, Amy, sometimes your superior intelligence is going to make it hard for you to understand the silly fads and hobbies that your peers enjoy. You'll just have to learn to deal with that."

"Yeah, I know," she said dully. She'd already heard this from her mother. "I'll see you later, Dr. Dave."

Hanging up, she went back into the living room and stared out the window at nothing in particular. So it wasn't the Cocodoodles after all. Unless, maybe, the candy contained some chemical so rare and exotic that the hospital tests couldn't identify it. She wondered if she should bring Cocodoodles to some major research laboratory.

From the window, she saw a couple of classmates leaving Monica's. Then a car pulled up, and four more got out and headed for her neighbor's door. They all wore those vacant, bland smiles. . . .

A thought hit her. Was it possible that Monica's treatments were doing something to the kids to make them act like zombies? No, it wasn't like Monica had personally treated all the kids at Amy's school. But what if . . . what if whatever Monica was doing to her patients, whatever those treatments and therapies consisted of . . . what if it was contagious? What if she hypnotized a student, and then that student was able to hypnotize other students?

But Monica isn't a bad person, Amy argued with herself. She would never do anything to harm another person.

Not *intentionally*. But what if Monica didn't realize that her treatments were dangerous? Amy had to know more about what was going on in there.

Her mother wouldn't be home until almost ten. So Amy was free to do a little spying. And as soon as the sun went down, she made her move. She went out the back way so that she could approach Monica's house without being seen by any of the patients who were coming and going. Fortunately, she'd been in that house many times and knew exactly where Monica had to be conducting her sessions. She crept along the side of the house until she reached the window of the guest bedroom.

Of course, the window was closed, and a curtain was drawn across the glass. But the curtain was made of gauze, and while it obscured the view for most people, Amy had her advanced eyesight to rely on. She peered through the gauze, and although she didn't have a totally clear view, she could see what was going on inside.

Monica had decorated the space with soft, drapey fabrics on the walls and glow-in-the-dark stars on the ceiling. Candles of all sizes stood all over the place, flickering in the semidark room. On the floor lay huge, fat cushions.

As Amy watched, the door of the room opened and Monica came in, escorting a girl Amy recognized from her French class, Tracee Bell. Not the world's brightest girl, but basically nice.

Monica hit a button on a tape player, and some jingling electronic music filled the room. She directed Tracee to sit on a certain cushion, and then she went to a cabinet, from which she selected some little bottles. From what Amy could see, she was weighing and measuring powders from different bottles and mixing them on a plate. A match was struck, and suddenly the plate held a flame. Monica placed a lid on the plate for a second, then removed it. The flame was gone, but the powders glowed like embers, and wisps of smoke drifted up.

Monica brought the plate with her and sat on the pillow facing Tracee. Amy pressed her ear closer to the glass so she could hear what was being said.

"Breathe deeply, Tracee. Let the aroma of the incense fill you until every part of your body is aware of the scent."

Tracee giggled. "You mean, like, my toes are supposed to smell the incense?"

"Let your breath out slowly," Monica continued. "Close your eyes. Listen to the music. Can you hear the waterfall?"

"No, I just hear a lot of techno stuff."

"Don't answer me, Tracee, just listen, and see the waterfall in your mind's eye. Let the music become the waterfall. You can be under that waterfall. You can feel cleansed of your insecurities."

"Is this going to make me neater? 'Cause my mother says I can have my own TV only if I keep my room clean. Only I keep forgetting to hang up my clothes."

"If you are feeling secure with yourself, everything improves," Monica intoned. "Stay very quiet, be very still. Concentrate on my voice."

Monica began to chant. It sounded like gibberish to Amy, though it might have been another language. It was actually a pretty sound, kind of soothing, like a lullaby. Every now and then, Monica would say something like "You are in touch with your inner self" or "You are aware of what you can be."

Amy yawned and wondered if Tracee would simply fall asleep.

"Open your eyes, Tracee."

Tracee did.

"Repeat after me," Monica said.

"Repeat after me," Tracee said, and Amy stifled a giggle.

"I am strong, I am invincible, I can be better than I am," Monica said.

"I am strong, I am invincible, I can be better than I am," Tracee repeated, and Amy didn't feel like giggling anymore. Tracee's voice was eerie. It was like a dead monotone, with no expression or inflection. Amy had heard Tracee speak lots of times, and this didn't sound like Tracee at all.

Monica spoke again. "I will be neat. I will pick up my clothes. I will keep my room clean."

"I will be neat. I will pick up my clothes. I will keep my room clean."

It went on like this for ten or fifteen minutes. It was very clear to Amy that Tracee was in a trance. Amy was sure that if Monica ordered Tracee to jump up and down and cluck like a chicken, she'd do it.

The whole business was giving Amy the creeps. It seemed as if Monica was casting a spell on Tracee, and Monica held the power to make Tracee do anything. And what exactly was in that incense? What was Tracee really breathing in so deeply?

Maybe it *was* Monica who was responsible for all the strangeness. But what was Amy going to do about it?

How could she convince Monica that she had to stop all this hypnosis business? Or maybe Monica would have to hypnotize them all again to get them back to normal.

"Amy Candler, what do you think you're doing?"

Amy practically jumped out of her own skin. "Monica!"

Her neighbor stood outside the back door of her house. "I could see you through those curtains, Amy. What are you doing, spying on me?"

There was no point in lying. "Yes," Amy said. "I've been wondering what you really do in there."

"Well then, why didn't you just ask me? Come on in."

Amy followed Monica inside and into the guest bedroom, where the electronic music played and the fumes of the incense made her want to cough. Tracee still sat there, mumbling, "I will be neat, I will be neat, I will pick up my clothes, I want that TV, I will be neat."

"Now, as you can see, I've placed Tracee in a mild hypnotic trance," Monica told Amy. "It's not that hard; I just use electronic music and lavender aroma to put her in a relaxed state. Then, while she's hypnotized, I make a suggestion as to how she can make a change in her life, or whatever she wants. And hopefully, when she wakes up, that suggestion will have become part of her subconscious and she'll find herself following the suggestion easily."

"*Too* easily," Amy said grimly. "Monica, this is dangerous! You're turning people into zombies!"

"Don't be silly," Monica scolded her. "Hypnosis is an accepted procedure. I've had some great success, helping people to relax or change bad habits. People tell me I have a talent, because my voice is so soothing."

Amy wasn't convinced. "But right now, you have a lot of power! I mean, you could tell Tracee to—to go out and kill someone!"

"Nonsense," Monica said. "Hypnosis can't make people do anything they don't already want to do. Watch." She took her position on the cushion facing Tracee. "Tracee, before you leave my house today, you must hop up and down on one leg for a full minute."

"I must hop up and down on one leg for a full minute," Tracee repeated.

"She repeats that," Monica told Amy, "but it doesn't mean anything to her. Really, Amy, what I'm doing is very normal. I'm developing a very good reputation. Groups have invited me to give demonstrations. In fact, I'm appearing at an assembly at your school on Friday, to talk to students about relaxing before a test. Now, I need to get back to my patient." She turned to Tracee.

"I want my own TV set."

"I want my own TV set," Tracee echoed.

"To get a TV set, I must keep my bedroom neat."

"To get a TV set, I must keep my bedroom neat."

"Good," Monica said. "Now, when I count to three, you will come out of your trance. One, two, three."

Tracee blinked. "Is it all over?"

"Yes," Monica said. "How do you feel?"

Tracee considered this. "I feel like going home and straightening up my room. Wow! I actually *want* to do that!"

"Excellent," Monica said. "Do you feel like hopping up and down on one foot?"

Tracee's brow wrinkled. "Why would I do a stupid thing like that?"

"Never mind," Monica said. She smiled triumphantly at Amy.

"Hi, Amy," Tracee said. "What are you doing here?"

Amy didn't know how to explain her presence. "Looking for answers" was the only thing she could think of to say.

"Well, you came to the right place!" Tracee declared. "Monica just solved my problem!"

Amy smiled but shook her head. She wasn't going to find the answer to *her* problem here.

nine

So it wasn't the Cocodoodles, and it wasn't Monica's treatments. It couldn't be the shoelaces; that fad was already on its way out. In-line skating—that was very popular. But how could skating transform normal teens into vacant zombies? Some chemical that was transmitted through the feet? No, that was ridiculous. Besides, all the students at Parkside didn't skate.

But something was making an awful lot of students behave in a very strange way, and it had to be something that a lot of students were involved in. Which left only one possibility. *Cherry Lane*.

But *how*? How could a very ordinary teen drama

change the way people behaved? When Amy's mother came home from teaching that evening, Amy brought up the subject.

"Television can have a lot of influence on people, can't it?"

Her mother was searching the refrigerator. "It certainly can. That's why parents don't want their children to watch so much."

"But what kind of influence can it have?" Amy persisted. "I remember a show that was on a couple of years ago. The main character wore her hair in a long braid, and suddenly everyone at school was braiding their hair. And what about that show where the girl kept saying 'as if!' Remember that?"

Nancy groaned. "Don't remind me. I thought that if you said 'as if' to me one more time, I'd go nuts."

"And there are fashion styles that kids pick up from TV," Amy went on. "So I guess it wouldn't be that weird if kids started picking up other stuff too. Like the way characters act."

"Yay, leftover tuna noodle casserole!" her mother exclaimed. "Did I make this two days ago or three? I wonder if it could be spoiled."

"Mom, what do you think? Can a person's behavior be influenced by TV?"

"I'm not sure, sweetie. People are always wondering if watching violence on TV makes children more violent. But there's no scientific proof. Amy, smell this. Is it still okay?"

Amy used her supersensitive ability and sniffed the glass bowl. "It's fine, Mom." How frustrating was this? Here she was worried about students turning into puppets, and her mother was worrying about tuna noodle casserole.

But even if *Cherry Lane* could influence viewers' behaviors, that still didn't explain anything. The characters on *Cherry Lane* didn't act like perfect, studious, well-behaved teens. If the kids at Parkside were really trying to imitate Brianna and Jenny and Tucker and all those guys, they'd just be falling in and out of love with each other.

Then Amy thought of another way the program could have an impact. An even more sinister method of changing how people behaved. Only, she didn't know if it was scientifically possible. It sounded a little too much like fantasy.

She didn't dare ask her mother. Any question would make Nancy suspicious, and Amy would have to suffer through another long lecture on how she should be more open-minded and less judgmental about her peers. So she saved her theory till the morning, when she arrived at school early and went to see Mr. Moran, the biology teacher.

"Mr. Moran, I heard that computer screens and mobile phones can transmit dangerous radiation," she said. "Like, you could get a brain tumor or something."

The biology teacher smiled. "That was a concern at one time, but it was proved false. Any level of radiation that exists is too small to have an impact."

"Well, what about a TV?" Amy wanted to know. "Can it transmit radiation? Like, if you're exposed to a TV for a long time, can it affect your mind?"

"Yes, it can," Mr. Moran replied, and Amy felt a spark of hope.

"It can make you stupid," Mr. Moran continued. His words doused the spark. It didn't extinguish her theory completely, though. There could be other ways *Cherry Lane* was manipulating her classmates.

She went to her homeroom, where her classmates, the humanoids, were studying quietly as they waited for the bell. Ms. Weller arrived and took roll, and once again there was perfect attendance. Then the intercom came on.

"Boys and girls, we have a very exciting announcement to make this morning. Our very own Parkside

Middle School has been selected to host the premiere of *Cherry Lane: The Movie* this Friday afternoon!"

Amy expected to hear the entire school erupt in cheers and squeals. But these new, perfect students just smiled and clapped politely. A cold chill began to travel up Amy's spine. If a TV show could have such a huge impact on her classmates, what could a movie do to them?

She went up to Ms. Weller's desk. "Ms. Weller, could I have a pass to go to the office? I want to see Dr. Noble about something."

Fortunately, Ms. Weller liked Amy and trusted her, so she didn't ask any questions. "Of course, Amy," she said, and handed her a pass.

For once, Dr. Noble was available and Amy didn't have to wait. She was ushered right into the office, where the principal was sitting behind her desk.

"Yes, what can I do for you?" Dr. Noble asked.

At that moment, Amy realized that anything she could say would sound foolish. But she had to give it a shot. "It's about *Cherry Lane: The Movie*."

The principal nodded. "It's very exciting, isn't it?"

"Actually . . . well . . . I don't think we should have the premiere here."

Dr. Noble's eyebrows went up. "Why not?"

"Well . . . um . . . you're always saying that we need to concentrate on getting educated, right? And how everything that goes on at school should be educational, right? So—so I don't think we should watch this movie during school hours. Because there's nothing educational about it."

Dr. Noble frowned slightly, but Amy could tell the principal was thinking, so she quickly followed up with an example.

"Remember back in October, when you asked the students to suggest assembly topics and guest speakers? Somebody asked if we could have a beautician come in and talk about cosmetics and hairstyles. And you said no, because it wasn't educational. So maybe we shouldn't be watching a movie like this in school either."

Dr. Noble smiled. "Perhaps I've been too strict in this regard. You're right, of course, that *Cherry Lane: The Movie* isn't exactly an educational experience. But you students have been behaving so well lately that I think you're due for a treat. And it's not as if this could possibly be a harmful experience."

"But it *is*!" Amy cried out. "It *is* harmful!"

Dr. Noble was taken aback by her outburst.

"How do you mean?"

Amy struggled to come up with an explanation. "It's . . . it's not good for us. It's doing stuff to us."

"You mean the show is having a bad influence on our students?" Dr. Noble considered that. "I've watched the show several times, and I agree, the stories put too much emphasis on romantic relationships between teenagers. But that's what you young people are interested in, isn't it? And I've been pleased to note that there's no violence on the program, no glorification of drugs or alcohol, and no foul language." She rustled through some papers. "It's been approved by Positive Control, you know." She showed Amy the paper with the list of approved TV shows, movies, and music. "In fact, the competition to host the premiere was sponsored by Positive Control."

That was another thing that seemed strange to Amy. Monday was the first they'd heard that the movie would have its premiere at a middle school. On Tuesday, only yesterday, people had begun collecting signatures for their petitions. Today was only Wednesday. How could the competition have been held and completed so fast?

She wanted to bring this to the principal's attention, but Dr. Noble was rising from her desk and looking at her watch. "I'm sorry, Amy, but I think we'll go on with our little movie premiere. And may I add a personal note? I advise you not to tell any of your friends and classmates that you've been to see me about this. You could become very unpopular!"

She already was. As the day progressed, Amy couldn't help noticing how people were avoiding her and eyeing her strangely. They were polite to her and no one said anything mean—their new personalities wouldn't let them be nasty. But they were definitely staying out of her way. Even Tasha, her best friend in all the world, blew her off. When Amy arrived at their usual table in the cafeteria, for the first time ever Tasha hadn't saved a seat for her.

And Eric was no different. Amy tried to corner him after school, but when some of his buddies approached, he walked away, as if he was ashamed to be seen talking to her.

But Amy couldn't allow herself time to feel depressed. She had a mission. Normally she would have asked Tasha and Eric to accompany her, but not this time. So she called to mind the address she'd memorized earlier from the paper on Dr. Noble's desk, looked on a map, and went to catch a bus that would take her to the office of Positive Control.

ten 10

I t was a very ordinary office building, one of those new modern ones, twenty stories high, with lots of glass and shiny metal. In the lobby, ordinary people milled around, getting off and on elevators. There was a uniformed man behind a desk, but he didn't pay any attention to Amy as she went to a big board on a wall that named all the businesses in the building and their locations.

The list was arranged alphabetically, and she went to the *Ps*. Parker, Eugene, Certified Public Accountant . . . Peterson and Myers, Law Firm . . . Planet Employment Agency . . . Positive Control, Inc.

Nothing gave her any clues as to what kind of business Positive Control was. But there was a location: Suite 523.

She took the elevator up to the fifth floor. If the company was doing something bad or illegal, it wasn't trying to hide—the office was directly across from the elevator and the sign on the door was clear: POSITIVE CONTROL, INC.: EDUCATIONAL SYSTEMS. A note beside it read, PLEASE RING BELL AND WAIT FOR BUZZER. So Amy did, and when she heard the buzzer she walked in.

There was nothing strange in here, either. Amy found herself in a small reception area, neatly furnished with a modern sofa and two chairs around a coffee table. There were serious-looking magazines on the coffee table, and Amy's eyes swept over them: *Education Today*, *Youth and Society*, *Contemporary Teacher*.

At a chrome desk, a young woman looked up from her computer screen. "Yes? May I help you?" she asked with a professional smile.

Now Amy wished she'd taken one of Monica's confidence treatments. "Uh . . . I want to talk to someone."

"Do you have an appointment?"

"Not really. I mean, no."

"Who do you want to talk to?"

"I'm not sure."

The woman continued to smile, but she was beginning to look a little impatient and Amy couldn't blame her. She tried to be more specific.

"I want to talk to someone about *Cherry Lane.*"

Immediate comprehension came to the receptionist's face, along with a slight weariness, as if she'd been asked this question too many times. She shook her head.

"I'm sorry, dear, but you see, the actors are not here. Positive Control is a consultant for the series. The show isn't produced in this building. It's filmed in Pasadena, and you won't have any luck going there for autographs either. There's an army of guards to protect the actors from their groupies."

Amy drew herself up stiffly. "I am *not* a groupie," she informed the woman.

"Well, whatever," the woman said. "Now, we do have a publicity packet that contains photographs of your favorite stars." She started toward a file cabinet, but her telephone buzzed, and she came back to the desk to answer it. "Yes? All right, I'm coming." She headed back toward the offices.

"What about my packet?" Amy asked.

"You'll have to wait," the woman called over her shoulder, and disappeared.

Amy drummed her fingers on the desk. She didn't see much point in waiting, but as long as she had the office to herself, she decided to do a little investigating, although she doubted she'd find anything of significance.

She went to the file cabinet and selected a drawer at random. Opening it, she saw a row of neatly filed folders with uninteresting labels. LANGUAGE ARTS—METHODS OF TEACHING; LINGUISTICS—RESEARCH IN; LITERACY RATES—TABLES AND FIGURES. She poked into a couple of the folders, and the contents appeared to be exactly as boring as the titles. The other drawers revealed nothing better.

With her ears alert for the sound of approaching footsteps, Amy continued her search. The file drawer in the receptionist's desk contained employment records. The other drawer held office supplies—staples, paper clips, that sort of thing.

There was a box of computer diskettes and CDs on the desk. She was just considering whether or not to slip one into the computer drive when she heard footsteps out by the elevator. Quickly she slammed the drawer as the door opened.

A young man in a motorcycle jacket entered. He wore a large messenger bag over one shoulder. "Hey, where's Pat?" he asked.

That had to be the name of the receptionist. "She's

out," Amy said, and on an impulse, she added, "I'm watching the desk."

"Oh. Well, here it is." He tossed a large brown envelope onto the desk.

"Here *what* is?" Amy asked.

"How should I know? It's the delivery I make from the Pasadena studio every day. Sign here." He thrust a paper at her.

Amy scribbled on the sheet. The guy didn't even glance at it as he shoved it into his messenger bag and strode out of the office.

In the silence that followed his departure, Amy stared at the package. Then she felt it. It was easy enough to identify the contents that way. The envelope contained a videotape.

Unfortunately, her genetically enhanced skills didn't include X-ray vision. Did she dare open the package and examine the contents more closely? What if Pat the receptionist came back?

There wasn't much Pat could do to her besides yell and scold and throw her out of the office. Amy was just a kid; the receptionist wouldn't call the police on her. Amy could always pretend she'd thought the package contained something of interest to a *Cherry Lane* groupie.

Using her fingernails, she pried open the staples that secured the envelope, and pulled out the tape. It was clearly labeled. *Cherry Lane*, episode 18. And there was an air date, which indicated that this particular episode would be on TV tomorrow. But what really intrigued her was a word that had been scrawled in pencil on a corner of the label: *enhanced.*

Amy looked around the room. There was no TV or VCR there. So here was a real test for her acute vision—could she see the actual frames on the tape? With a finger she pulled some of the tape out and examined it closely.

It wasn't easy. She had to squint and stare at the brown tape until her eyes burned. But eventually she was able to make out the pictures. And by pulling the tape out fast, she actually got a jumpy image of the first scene in tomorrow's episode: Jenny talking on the telephone. Thrilling.

She pulled some more. Suddenly she felt a little twinge in her forehead, that almost-headache she got every time she saw the show. She held the tape closer to her eyes. Now the images were blurred, but as she continued to strain and squint, she began to make out individual frames. Jenny on the telephone, Jenny on the telephone, Jenny on the telephone, Jenny on the telephone—no, wait, there was a frame between those last two that wasn't a picture of anyone.

There were letters on the frame. The more she strained, the more her head hurt, but she didn't give up until the letters formed words that she could read.

You will be punctual.

What was that supposed to mean? She pulled out more tape, examining frames until she found another one with words.

You will do your homework.

A few frames later she found *You will eat what you are given without complaint.* Then there was a gap where the frames showed Jenny hanging up the phone, but eventually there was another word frame: *You will be polite.*

She began pulling the tape out faster. Now that her eyes were adjusting to the task, the headache faded and the word frames were easier to find.

You will obey your parents and your teachers.

You will not fight.

You will speak softly.

You will smile.

You will not run.

It went on like that. At irregular intervals throughout the tape, there were similar statements. As Amy fingered the tape, her sensitive touch could actually make out where the tape had been cut and the message frames spliced in.

She was so caught up in searching and feeling and reading that she missed the sound of the footsteps. Suddenly the door swung open, and Pat the receptionist stood there.

"What do you think you're doing?" she cried out in alarm.

Amy dropped the tape. And despite the instructions she'd just read, she *ran*.

eleven

"They're called subliminal messages," Monica told Amy when she heard about the frames in the tape. "It was used way back, years ago, in movies. Advertisers thought that if a picture of a soda was inserted among the frames, the movie audience wouldn't realize that they'd seen it because it went by too fast. But they would subconsciously recognize the picture, and it would make them thirsty, so they would go out to the lobby and buy something to drink."

"And that really worked?" Amy asked.

"I don't think so," Monica said. "Personally, I think it sounds more like science fiction."

"But, Monica, haven't you noticed any difference in people lately? Tasha and Eric, for example, or any of my classmates."

Monica smiled and nodded. "They seem more relaxed. I'd like to think I've had something to do with that."

Amy could see that she wouldn't be any more successful in explaining her concerns to Monica than she'd been in trying to explain them to her mother and Dr. Noble. They *liked* the kids' new personalities.

But if they all knew what was making the kids behave this way, surely they wouldn't be so enthusiastic. What Positive Control was doing couldn't be right. They were manipulating minds, influencing people to act in ways they might not normally act. They were brainwashing kids, taking away their free will, preventing them from making their own decisions. It had to be illegal.

The TV show had done some serious damage to Amy's friends and classmates. She shuddered at the thought of what a large-screen movie could do to them.

What she needed now was evidence, something real that she could show them to prove what she knew. She could have kicked herself for not hanging on to the tape when she ran out of the Positive Control office.

But she could make another tape. Tomorrow was

Thursday. She would tape the episode of *Cherry Lane,* and on Friday she would bring the tape to school. There was a VCR at school that could click on a tape frame by frame—teachers used it to stop a video when there was something they wanted a class to study. Amy would show them all what Positive Control was doing to people. There was no way Dr. Noble would allow the movie to be shown.

Back home, she asked her mother if they had any blank videotapes in the house.

"There's a package of three that I bought on sale, in the closet," her mother told her. "But I hope you're not planning to tape anything off our TV."

"Why?"

"I finally realized why we're having so much trouble taping shows. It's not because we're both too stupid to figure out how to use the new remote control."

"You mean there's something wrong with the remote control?"

Her mother nodded. "It's defective. I'll have to bring it to the store and get it fixed, or exchange it."

"When?" Amy demanded. "Now?"

Her mother looked at her as if she was nuts. "Amy, I just got home, I'm tired! I'm not going to race out to get a remote control fixed."

"But, Mom—"

Her mother was adamant. "There is nothing on TV that could be so important it absolutely has to be taped." She looked at her watch. "Besides, the store would be closed by now."

Amy couldn't argue with that. Vaguely she considered sneaking out and breaking into the store to find a replacement remote control. But most stores had iron bars to prevent just such activities. And while she might be physically superior to most people, she wasn't Wonder Woman.

Somehow she would have to get the remote control fixed before four-thirty tomorrow, when *Cherry Lane* came on. School let out at three-forty. Even if she used her super-speed, she wouldn't be able to make it to the store, exchange the remote control, and get home in time to tape the program. And it wouldn't do her any good to tape Friday's show. By then it would be too late. Whatever damage could be done to the kids by the movie would already have been done.

She tried to imagine what the movie could do. Destroy any last spark of individuality or personality? Erase all emotions? Turn kids into actual robots that could function only in response to commands?

And even then, would the adults think anything was wrong?

Amy had to save her peers, and there was only one way she could do it. She had to get the proof—no matter how much danger it put her in.

Cutting classes was a pretty big crime at Parkside. Even sneaking away from school at lunchtime to find something edible at the local fast-food joints was against the rules. Still, Amy wasn't too worried. Things had been so peaceful lately at Parkside, the hall monitors were probably pretty relaxed and not watching the doors all that carefully. She couldn't walk out between classes—too many people would notice. She decided she'd ask for a rest room pass during French, her second-to-last class of the day, and take off then.

What little feeling was left in the students at Parkside was visible on Thursday. There was actually a small ripple of excitement about the movie premiere tomorrow. In the old days, they would have been wild and crazy, Amy thought wistfully. Turmoil, commotion, teachers complaining that the students wouldn't settle down. Now the slight increase in the volume of their voices probably wouldn't even register on a sound monitor.

For the zillionth time, Amy checked in her bag to make sure she had the remote control and the receipt from the store where her mother had purchased it.

Since Amy had given all her money to Eric, she couldn't buy a new one, but she assumed that the store would fix it or replace it for free.

The bell had just rung in her French class, and Amy went to the teacher's desk. *"Madame Duquesne, est-ce que je peux aller aux toilettes?"*

The teacher frowned slightly, probably because Amy could have used the rest room during the break between classes. But she didn't make a big fuss about it and gave Amy a pass.

Making sure she had her bag with her, Amy went out into the hall. She passed a hall monitor, who smiled at her. Amy returned her bland smile and flapped the pass in the air to show that she had permission to be there. The monitor nodded. Amy reached the end of the hall and was about to turn toward the exit when the monitor called out to her.

"The rest room is there," the girl said.

"What?" Amy asked, looking back.

"You have a rest room pass," the monitor said. "And you just walked right past the rest room."

"Oh. How dumb of me." Amy went into the rest room. Inside, she counted to fifty, then came back out. The monitor smiled at her again. Amy smiled back and again started walking toward the end of the hall.

"You're going in the wrong direction," the monitor

called to her. "You came from that classroom," and she pointed in the opposite direction. Amy took a deep breath and broke into a run.

She knew the monitor wouldn't be able to catch her. And of course, she would report Amy, and tomorrow Amy would be in trouble. But by then Amy would have the evidence to show Dr. Noble, and she was willing to get into trouble to save her classmates.

She could hear the hall monitor's feet pounding behind her, but they were too far away for her to be concerned. The exit door was only a few yards in front of her.

But it was blocked. By the irate figure of her principal.

"Exactly *what* is going on here?" Dr. Noble demanded.

twelve

Amy was the only person in the school cafeteria, except for some teacher she didn't know. He sat at another table with a stack of papers he was grading, and he basically ignored her. But he knew she was there, and he wouldn't let her leave anytime soon.

Every now and then he glanced at her with a look that was not friendly. She couldn't blame him. She was the reason he had to sit there. Teachers had become accustomed to not having to serve detention duty. Amy was the first student in almost two weeks to be punished like this.

Dr. Noble had been very upset. "We were setting a

record here at Parkside," she'd admonished Amy. "Almost two weeks with no one committing an infraction! How could you do this?"

There was no trial, and Amy wasn't given any opportunity to defend herself—which wouldn't have done any good anyway, since no one would have believed her. She was sentenced to ten days of after-school detention, to begin immediately. Given the seriousness of her infraction, a little something extra had been thrown in too. Amy would not be allowed to join her classmates in watching the premiere of *Cherry Lane: The Movie*.

So she hadn't been able to take the remote control into the shop for repair or exchange. She hadn't even been home in time to catch the episode. And today, Friday, at this very moment, her friends and her classmates were being subjected to what Amy feared could be very intense brainwashing. There was a very good chance that people Amy knew, and people Amy loved, would never be the same.

Her eyes filled with tears as she envisioned Tasha, her very best friend in all the world. And when she thought about Eric, the tears began to fall.

The teacher grading the papers noticed this. He misinterpreted her tears, and he wasn't at all sympathetic. "Don't waste your time crying," he snapped. "You're not seeing the movie, and it's your own fault."

Amy strained, trying to hear what was going on in the movie. But the auditorium was way over on the other side of the building, and even super-ears didn't stretch that far. She looked at her watch. It was now forty-five minutes since the starting time of the movie, and the movie was two hours long. Under the watchful eye of this teacher, it was impossible for Amy to do anything. And it was probably too late anyway. Who knew what kind of damage had already been done to the students' minds?

But how could she just sit here while evil forces were at work? She looked around the room. She could try to make a run for the door, or the windows, but this teacher was twice her size and looked like he was in pretty good shape. She doubted she would make it very far. There had to be another option.

That was when she noticed a gaping hole in the ceiling, directly above a ladder near the cafeteria kitchens. There'd been some work going on lately, to fix the heating or the air-conditioning or something.

She raised her hand.

"What do you want?" the teacher asked.

"My legs are falling asleep," Amy complained. "Can I walk around and stretch them?"

He immediately became suspicious. "You're not getting out of this room, young lady."

"I won't go near the doors," Amy promised. "Or the windows. I'll just walk over to the kitchen entrance and back, that's all."

"You stay where you are," he ordered.

"Sir, I've been in detention before," Amy said indignantly. "We are allowed to get up and move around, once every hour."

The teacher looked at the clock. "You haven't been in here for an hour yet. In ten minutes you can walk to the kitchen door and back."

It was the best Amy could hope for. And she thought it was the longest ten minutes she'd ever experienced. But she spent them looking at the hole and the ladder.

"All right," the teacher said. "You can get up now and walk. But don't try anything stupid. I'll be watching you."

She rose slowly and gave a big yawn, as if trying to stretch. Casually she tossed her shoulder bag over her shoulder.

"You don't need to carry your bag to stretch your legs," the teacher barked.

Amy looked at him innocently. "This is my mother's rule. She says I should never leave my bag lying around. She says you can't trust anyone, not even teachers. You're not telling me to disobey my mother, are you?"

He looked annoyed, but he didn't force her to leave the bag. His eyes were on her as she ambled toward the kitchen door.

Even walking slowly, it took only a minute to get to the ladder. Through the hole, she could see the pipes that the workers had been fixing. She estimated the size of the hole, then glanced at the teacher, then looked back at the hole. She did some rapid figuring in her head.

"What are you looking at?" the teacher asked.

She couldn't waste another second. Springing like a cat, she leaped off the floor onto a rung of the ladder.

"Hey, stop that!" The teacher was on his feet. But Amy was scampering up the ladder, and within two seconds she had squeezed her body into the gaping hole, wrapping her arms around a pipe and using it to inch herself forward into the air-conditioning duct.

She could still hear the teacher yelling, but the sound was becoming fainter. She assumed he'd climbed the ladder after her, but she knew he wouldn't be able to fit through the hole.

She just hoped the pitch-black darkness and the musty smell wouldn't destroy her sense of direction. And that somewhere, at the other end of the building, there would be a way out.

thirteen 13

She could barely breathe. She took short gasps as she edged along the air-conditioning duct in the ceiling, trying not to think about where she was or what kind of nasty little creepy crawling creatures might be sharing this space with her. Silently she congratulated herself for having the foresight to wear jeans that morning and not her short, tight suede skirt.

She clung to the pipe. Thank goodness the weather had been warm and the air-conditioning had been on. The pipe was cool to the touch. Her ears were alert, but so far she hadn't heard anything. Then, very faintly, through layers of whatever ceilings were made out of, she caught a murmur.

The duct she was in divided. She listened carefully and crawled in the direction the murmur was coming from. She wasn't even sure if it was a voice—it could just have been a rumbling pipe. But as she got closer, she recognized the sound. It was a sound she'd know anywhere, since she'd heard it so many times.

Jenny, crying over Billy.

She wriggled ahead, faster now. Jenny's sobs were getting louder, but Amy didn't know whether that was because she was getting closer to the auditorium or because Jenny was crying harder. Then she saw a bit of light.

It came from a grating, and she made her way onto it. Peering through the tiny holes, she saw only a floor, and she knew she wasn't directly over the auditorium. She figured she was probably in a hallway just outside it. Should she keep going and hope to find a way to drop down right in the middle of the auditorium? Or should she get out now and run the risk of being captured before she got the auditorium doors open?

She still didn't even know what she would do when—or if—she got into the room where the movie was being shown. But she did know that she'd been up in this ceiling for at least twenty minutes. She didn't have much time left.

She picked at the screws that held the grating in place; she wished she still had the fake fingernails she and Tasha had once applied. But in a way, those missing bits of plastic helped anyway—when she'd worn the fake nails, she hadn't been able to bite the real ones, and her own nails were longer and stronger now. She was able to get one into a screw head and twist it open.

She worked feverishly on all the screws, but even so, it took at least ten minutes to loosen them all. Quietly she lifted the grating and peered down.

She *was* in the hall, just outside the auditorium. No sound was coming from the auditorium now, but that didn't mean the movie was over. Brianna was probably doing one of her long, faraway looks.

Amy twisted her body around until her feet were just over the hole and eased herself out. Dangling from the grating, she found herself looking straight into the eyes of her neighbor, Monica.

Monica dropped the case she was carrying. "Amy!"

"Shhh!" Amy hissed.

But Monica was too startled to obey her command. "Amy, what's going on?" she cried out.

Amy dropped to the floor. She rushed past Monica to the door at the back of the auditorium.

The auditorium was still dark. On the screen in front of her, a gigantic Billy was talking to a mammoth Jenny.

"You were right," he was saying. "I was wrong. How could I have been such a fool? Here I've been searching for my one true love, only to find that she's been here all along. Right here on Cherry Lane."

"Oh, Billy," Jenny said.

Billy took her in his arms and they kissed. Dumbfounded, Amy shook her head. After all that, Billy and Jenny were going to end up together? What a totally stupid show.

Then she realized that the music was swelling and the camera was moving above the couple. It was the end of the movie. Even if she leaped onto the projector and smashed it, it would be too late.

Unless . . . unless . . .

She fumbled in her bag and pulled out the broken remote control. Just because the taping feature was broken, that didn't mean that all the remote control features wouldn't work. Desperately she raised it and pointed it toward the screen. And she hit Rewind.

The camera began to go lower until the screen was filled with Jenny and Billy locked in their embrace. They moved apart. Their lips moved, but only squeaky gibberish came out. Then they started moving back-ward, away from each other.

An odd rumbling sound began to echo in the audito-rium. People were mumbling, chairs were squeaking. Voices rose and became more shrill. Suddenly some-one let out a shriek. And the whole room exploded with anger.

It was a riot—and not a laugh riot, a real riot. Stu-dents were shouting, screaming, throwing books and whatever else they could get their hands on. A couple of boys started tearing down the curtains that hung on either side of the auditorium stage. Fights broke out, and the screaming increased. Someone pulled on a fire alarm. Frightened-looking teachers ran through the room, yelling at students to stop at once, to sit down. No one was paying any attention to them.

In horror, Amy watched one girl scratch another so hard that blood ran down the victim's cheek. A boy fell to the floor unconscious, knocked out by a blow to the head. Behind Amy, Monica was in shock. "Amy, what's going on?" she asked in bewilderment. "I came to do my relaxation presentation, and—"

Amy grabbed Monica's hand. "Come on!"

Thank goodness, this time Monica obeyed, and al-lowed herself to be dragged down one hall and up another until they reached the principal's office. The office was just across the hall from the cafeteria, and that nasty detention teacher was standing in the doorway. He jumped forward to block Amy's passage. "I've been looking for you!" he yelled.

Amy pushed him out of the way and pulled Monica into the office. She brought her around the secretary's desk to the control board for the intercom and flipped the switch for the auditorium. Through the open intercom, she could hear that the rampage in the auditorium was still going on.

"Quick!" she instructed Monica. "Start hypnotizing!" She opened Monica's briefcase and began searching through the little bottles.

Her voice quivering, Monica began to speak into the intercom. "You will relax. You will take deep breaths, so deep that you will feel like every part of your body is breathing. Your arms are breathing. Your hands are breathing. Your fingers . . ."

Amy didn't stick around to hear about the breathing fingers. With a bottle of lavender essence in her hand, she ran out of the office. The teacher tried to block her once more.

"Hey, you!" he yelled in outrage, but Amy pushed him aside. She figured that by now she'd probably racked up two years of detention anyway.

In the cafeteria, she scrambled up the ladder and into the gaping hole again. Once more she inched her way through the duct, although this time she moved a little faster, since she knew where she was going. When she got to the place where the duct divided, she moved in the opposite direction, hoping that the vent she could now see was the one that led directly into the auditorium. She emptied the bottle of lavender essence, the scent that was supposed to calm people down, and the oil oozed through the little holes.

She would never know if it was the hypnosis, or the lavender, or a combination of both. Or maybe it was simply that the movie had completely rewound. But when she dropped down from the ceiling, in the hall by the auditorium, there was utter silence. The riot was over.

fourteen
14

In the parking lot outside Sunshine Square, on a bright and warm Sunday morning, the in-line skaters and the skateboarders were out in force. It had been almost two weeks since the Parkside Middle School riot, but people were still talking about it.

"I still don't understand why it was only Parkside that had the problems," Tasha said. "Teens everywhere watched *Cherry Lane*." It was her first time on in-line skates, and she clutched Amy with her right hand and Eric with her left as she wobbled along.

"The special enhanced episodes were only shown

through the cable system that operates in our neighborhood," Amy told her. "We were a test case."

"Gee," Eric said sarcastically. "Weren't we lucky? I still can't believe our own teachers, our principal, our *parents,* would let this go on."

Amy tried to be fair. "They didn't really understand what was happening. And I guess it was kind of a nice change, having kids who did everything right."

"And that Positive Control organization—it just wanted to make kids more well-behaved?" Tasha asked.

"I guess so," Amy said. "But maybe they had more serious motives. Maybe they wanted control so they could make us do . . . do . . . well, whatever they wanted. Pretty creepy, huh?"

"Very," Tasha agreed. "Hey, I'm falling!" Somehow Eric and Amy managed to keep her upright. Amy wished she could set Tasha down for a while so she could do some real skating. It was a lot easier and more fun for her and Eric now. Once Eric had come to his senses and realized what he'd done, he'd returned the VCR and used the money to buy decent secondhand skates for both of them.

Tasha must have read her thoughts. "I think I'll take a break," she said. Amy and Eric led her to the side of the parking lot, where some girls stood around talking. Tasha pulled a bag from her pocket.

"Anyone want an orange Cocodoodle?"

Linda Riviera looked at her in disdain. "Tasha, nobody eats Cocodoodles anymore. Where have you *been*?" From her bag she took out something called a Happy-snappy and unwrapped it. Of course, she didn't offer a bite to anyone. Linda was back to normal too.

Amy and Eric could now do some serious skating, and they flew across the lot. Amy passed Alan Greenfield on his skateboard. He made a face at her.

"Eat a booger, Amy Candler!"

Amy skidded to a stop. "Alan Greenfield, you're disgusting! Eric, did you hear what he said to me?"

Eric was laughing. "Oh, don't be offended, everyone talks like that now. Haven't you seen *Fungal Retaliators*?"

"Fungal *what*?"

A passing classmate heard her. "Thursdays, nine o'clock, Channel Twelve, it's great!"

"It's about these cartoon characters who are always saying these gross things," Eric told her. "It's pretty funny."

Amy then noticed that several kids were wearing T-shirts that referred to either *Fungal Retaliators*, "boogers," "caca," or "doodoo." She'd make sure her TV wasn't tuned anywhere near Channel Twelve on Thursday nights.

Although she'd probably end up watching the show

sooner or later. It was important to stay in touch with the latest fads.

Just then a skateboarder collided with an in-line skater. "You piece of crud!" one of them shrieked.

"Zit-face!" the other yelled back.

The words were music to Amy's ears. Parkside Middle School was back to normal.

Don't miss

replica

#16

Happy Birthday, Dear Amy

Amy's birthday is coming up. She's turning thirteen. Now she'll be an official teenager—and she wants to celebrate with a real blowout. But on the big day, Amy wakes up and is definitely *not* ready to party.

Her appearance is somewhat unexpected.

Her growing pains have taken on . . . well, unusual proportions.

Her family and friends don't know what to do.

Amy may be an extraordinary girl, but can she ever be just a normal teenager?